Loud laughter filled the tunnel

Dropping into a combat crouch, the soldier moved to the opening and risked a peek. A spacious chamber had been carved from the salt. Stacked within were the bundles of cocaine unloaded from the speedboat. Rabican had a cache any drug dealer would drool over. Enough to keep the entire country in coke for the next decade.

Rabican wasn't in the chamber but four of his flunkies were. They had finished unloading and were standing around awaiting orders.

Bolan edged backward and froze. A hard object had gouged him in the back of the head.

He immediately recognized it as the muzzle of a gun.

MACK BOLAN ®
The Executioner

DON PENDLETON'S
EXECUTIONER®
THE
SCORPION RISING

A GOLD EAGLE BOOK FROM
WORLDWIDE.®

TORONTO • NEW YORK • LONDON
AMSTERDAM • PARIS • SYDNEY • HAMBURG
STOCKHOLM • ATHENS • TOKYO • MILAN
MADRID • WARSAW • BUDAPEST • AUCKLAND

First edition May 2003
ISBN 0-373-64294-6

Special thanks and acknowledgment to
David Robbins for his contribution to this work.

SCORPION RISING

O Liberty, how many crimes are committed in thy name?

—Roland

A wiser man than I once said, "Give me liberty or give me death." I will use everything in my power to preserve America's freedom.

—Mack Bolan

To Judy, Joshua and Shane.

Prologue

Kazakhstan, eighteen months ago

The sentries on perimeter duty were making a circuit of the fence. Although it was against regulations one had a cigarette in his mouth. The other was telling a joke about a farmer's daughter and a tractor salesman. He stopped in amazement when he saw the barbed wire atop the fence had been cut.

"Sergei, look!" were the last words the soldier ever uttered.

Two soft sounds punctuated his exclamation, the *chuff-chuff* of a weapon fitted with a sound suppressor. Each sentry acquired a hole in the center of his forehead, then fell without an outcry. Before they hit the ground a pair of shadows caught the bodies and quietly lowered the dead soldiers and their AK-47s to the hard earth.

Two more shadows joined the first pair. Exhibiting mil-

itary precision and skill, they went over the fence. At a hand
signal from the slimmest of the quartet, they fanned out in
a skirmish line and catfooted toward a large building at the
center of the compound. Laughter from a barracks located
adjacent to it brought them to an abrupt halt. They
crouched, SMGs ready. Two were armed with M-4s fitted
with sound suppressors and night-vision optics, one with
an M-249. The fourth, the slimmest, had a slung Remington Model 870 combat shotgun. Three of them wore 9 mm
Steyr S-Series semiauto pistols in holsters on their right
hips. The slim one favored a Glock. In all other respects
the four figures were virtually identical; their blacksuits,
their lightweight mesh ski masks, even their black shoes
were the same.

At the building the slim one paused before a door and
gingerly tested the knob. Another hand signal, and the four
specters glided down a narrow corridor, the slim one on
point.

Midway down light spilled from an open doorway. The
four were making toward it when suddenly another door
directly in front of them opened and out stepped a burly
man with a cup of steaming coffee in one hand and a piece
of sausage in the other. He blinked in surprise and opened
his mouth to shout a warning.

The slim intruder was a blur. One hand clamped onto
the man's mouth while the other swept in an arc and buried
the five-inch blade of a spring-loaded, doubled-edged knife
in his right eye socket. The man gave a convulsive shudder, gurgled briefly and died on his feet.

The body was carefully lowered. Again the quartet warily advanced. As they neared the open door they heard
someone humming.

A squat, balding officer sat behind an oak desk that had

seen better days. His combat boots were propped on top amid a sprawl of paperwork, and he was thumbing through a girlie magazine. He opened the centerfold, whistled softly and smacked his lips.

"Colonel Gorno?"

On hearing his name the officer glanced up. He saw a slim figure in his doorway and a larger one behind it, holding an M-4 trained squarely on his head. Gorno turned to stone. "Who are you? How did you get in here? What do you want?"

"You've been naughty, Colonel," the slim figure said. "You've been selling high-tech arms on the black market."

"I have done no such thing," Gorno blustered. "Who sent you? That accent. You are not Russian."

"I'm from the land of the free and the home of the brave," the slim figure said glibly, "where some people in high places are very upset with you."

Gorno licked his thick lips and set down the magazine. "Whoever you are," he said, spreading his hands palms out, "surely an arrangement can be worked out? There is no need for anything drastic."

"That's where you're wrong," the slim figure responded, and nodded at the large man with the M-4.

The rear of Colonel Alexi Gorno's cranium burst outward, showering the wall behind him with brains, hair and gore.

The slim intruder laughed and remarked in English, "Not bad for our first outing, boys. I think I can get to like this."

Paris, France, six months ago

LOCATED ON THE Avenue de Grenelle, the corporate headquarters of Perigord Industries towered fifteen stories into

the crisp Parisian air. For security reasons only two en-
trances existed. Visitors used the front lobby, blissfully
unaware their features and movements were monitored by
closed-circuit video cameras. Employees were required to
use a small entrance at the rear. Typically, between seven-
thirty and eight a.m. was the busiest half hour of the day
for the uniformed guards whose job it was to check every
ID and refuse admittance to anyone not on their list.

Security was tight at Perigord. It had to be. As one of
the leading chemical manufacturers worldwide, Perigord
was often the target of industrial espionage.

On this particular morning a line formed, as it invari-
ably did. The security guards scrutinized every ID card. But
in an effort to hurry things along they weren't quite as dili-
gent as they were at less busy times of the day. A quick
glance and the worker was permitted to file through.

Patiently waiting her turn was a slim woman in her
midtwenties. Lustrous auburn hair framed an oval face
notable for its smooth complexion and a pair of piercing
jade eyes. She smiled at the young guard who took her ID
and said in perfect French, "Good morning. You must be
new. I don't recall seeing you before."

Flattered by her attention, the young man barely gave
her identification card a glance.

"You're the one who must be new, Mademoiselle
Racine. I have worked for Perigord for three years now."
He handed her card back with a flourish and an inviting
smile. "Perhaps we will see each other again soon?"

"That would be nice." Racine bestowed a smile of her
own, one that would melt a candle at twenty paces. She
whisked by the security station and into one of four elevators already half-full. Men moved aside to make room,
some openly ogling her. Impervious to their lechery, she

pushed the button for the twelfth floor and stood with her hands clasped in front of her stylish dress as the elevator filled and then whined upward.

Only one other occupant was still in the car when it reached the twelfth floor. He was big and had exceptionally broad shoulders, and if anyone had looked closely, they would have noticed his blond hair had brown roots and his blond mustache wasn't completely flush against his skin at the left end of his mouth.

Their eyes met, and Racine grinned. "Relax, Carson." Her English was as impeccable as her French. "You look as if someone shoved a broomstick up your ass."

"I don't like this kind of op, and you know it," the man responded. He stiffly pried at the knot to his tie. "I don't like wearing monkey suits, either. Give me a uniform any day."

A bell chimed and the elevator stopped. Carson motioned for Racine to precede him and they strolled down a plush hallway to a door on the right. Racine opened it without knocking. Inside were four people. Two were on the floor, bound hand and foot, blindfolded and gagged. The other two were their teammates. One was crew cut and wore a brown suit.

The other had curly dark hair and walked with the light spring of a tiger. He was immaculately dressed.

"We all set?" Racine asked. Both men nodded.

She stepped up to the pair of employees on the floor and bent low. "Your boss is scum," she said in French. "He deserves his fate. Remember that when the police question you later."

Faces became etched with fright and confusion.

In the hallway the quartet turned toward the stairwell. They smiled at workers they passed, and Racine greeted everyone with a hearty, *"Bonjour."* To all intents and purposes they were exactly as they seemed, four executives going about their daily business. No one thought to question them. New faces weren't cause for alarm in a company that employed more than three hundred personnel.

The stairwell was empty. The soft-soled shoes the men had on were silent as they climbed, but Racine's heels clicked with clockwork precision. She cracked open the door to the upper floor and scanned the hallway before committing herself. After her trailed the three men, their hands under their jackets.

They came to a conference room. Carson and the other two men filed past Racine. As they entered, they leveled the Heckler & Koch MP-5s their jackets had concealed, each fitted with a sound suppressor.

Fourteen members of Perigord's upper management were seated around an oval table. They were shocked speechless by the intrusion. A middle-aged man at the head of the table regained his composure and rose to demand, "Who are you? What is the meaning of this?"

"I don't speak French," Carson said, "but maybe this will get the point across." At his nod, he and his companions cut loose, spraying the room with lead at cyclic rates of 600 rounds per minute.

Riddled where they sat, the men and women at the table never made an outcry. Their bodies jerked and thrashed to multiple impacts as the mahogany table and the walls were spattered with scarlet. The middle-aged man who had stood was flung back against his chair, and both crashed to the floor but not loud enough to be heard beyond the room's confines.

It was over almost as soon as it began. Carson and his stone-faced associates ejected spent magazines and fed in new ones, then slid the submachine guns under their jackets and exited.

Racine was waiting, her eyes on the thin gold-plated watch on her wrist. "We're right on schedule, boys," she whispered and moved toward another door farther down. This time only she went in. The others were to stay outside and cover her.

A petite secretary glanced up from a computer screen. "May I help you?"

"I have an appointment to see Monsieur Perigord," Racine said.

"You do?" the secretary said uncertainly. "I am aware of no such appointment." She swiveled her chair to consult a date book and flipped a couple of pages. "What is your name, please?"

"Alice in Wonderland," Racine replied, sliding up behind the chair. By then she had a garrote in her hands, and as the pretty secretary twisted to look up, Racine applied it with lightning speed and precision, cutting off the woman's breath. Planting herself, she tensed both arms and went into her kill.

The secretary gave a frightened bleat. She tried to rise, but Racine pressed on her shoulders. The woman clawed at the garrote with growing urgency, and when that failed, she tried to rake her fingernails across Racine's face and eyes. Racine butted her hands away. Then, with startling suddenness, it was over. The secretary lay on her side on the wine-red carpet, her tongue protruding, her countenance contorted in a grotesque mockery of her former loveliness.

Coldly, methodically, Racine unwound the garrote, wiped it on the other's blouse and straightened. Slipping it into her purse, she smoothed her dress and walked into the inner sanctum.

Marcel Perigord was on the phone, his chair turned so he could gaze out over the picturesque Paris scenery. He didn't hear her come in. Racine heard him say, "The shipment must be there by the tenth of the month. Our client was quite specific. He is also quite temperamental. If the tanker doesn't dock on time, he might withhold the rest of the payment. And we can't have that."

Racine sat on the edge of his huge desk and crossed her legs. Casually picking up a pen, she tapped it on a gold-embossed clock.

Perigord swung around his chair and did a double take. "What in the world?" he declared, then glanced toward the reception room. Covering the mouthpiece, he demanded, "Who are you and how did you get in here?"

"Today is the day, Marcel."

Perplexed, not knowing what to make of her, Perigord said into the mouthpiece, "Forgive me, Jean. I must go. I'll call you back in, say, five minutes."

"I wouldn't be so sure, if I were you," Racine commented as he hung up. "Life has a way of throwing nasty surprises our way when we least expect them."

"I repeat," Perigord said curtly, "who are you? Why did Miss Lavin let you in? I don't recall having any appointments until later this afternoon."

The woman shared the same smile that had melted the heart of the security guard. "Marcel, Marcel, Marcel. What are we to do with you? Only forty-three and suffering from premature senility."

Perigord's expression clouded. "I don't find you the least bit amusing, *mademoiselle*. If you don't explain yourself this instant I will have Miss Lavin call security."

"Can't punch that little button yourself, huh?" Racine leaned on her right hand and winked. "You're getting lazy and sloppy. Our people would never have caught on otherwise."

"Your people?" Perigord said, more confused than ever. "Caught on to what, might I inquire?"

"The fact your company has been selling illicit chemicals to Libya and Iraq. What were you thinking, Marcel? You don't need the money. You're as rich as old Midas."

All the color had drained from Perigord's face. "I don't know what you're talking about," he said defensively.

"Sure you do. Thanks to you, those two countries will soon have the capability to wage chemical warfare on an unprecedented scale unless something is done to stop the flow." Racine wagged a slender finger. "Naughty, naughty."

Perigord's eyes narrowed. "I understand now. You're a reporter, is that it? From one of those muckraking rags that are forever attacking big business."

"Oh, Marcel, please." Racine rose and slowly walked around the end of the desk.

She had slipped off her high heels before she rose and was now barefoot except for her nylons. "I'm all for capitalism. I like money as much as the next person. More so. It's why I'm about to do what I'm about to do."

"You make no sense whatsoever," Perigord stated angrily. "I have had enough of this nonsense." He reached for the intercom.

Rancine's right hand flashed in a palm heel strike that caught Marcel Perigord flush on the nose. Spurting blood, he tried to stand to defend himself, but he was too slow. Her second blow was a sword-hand slash across his throat that turned him a bright shade of purple. Darting behind him, she clamped her left forearm around his jaw and her right arm around the crown of his angular head. With a sharp, violent twist, she applied the coup de grâce, and at the crack of his spine, she stepped back with a satisfied grin.

Carson stood inside the doorway, and he was frowning. "Why didn't you just shoot the bastard?"

"I like to get up close and personal."

"You enjoy it too much, you know that, Maddy?" Carson grumbled. "Get it done so we can get the hell out of here."

Racine claimed her purse from the desktop. From it she extracted a standard business card, which she wedged partway into Perigord's mouth. "Nice touch, don't you think?"

A large black scorpion was imprinted on the card.

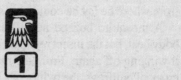

The Louisiana bayou country was famous for its treacherous marshes and swamps, its fearsome alligators and its colorful Cajuns. Of late, it had become notorious for a new element—a major ferrying point for drugs smuggled into the United States from Latin America. For months the government had worked to determine who was behind the operation. Only recently had it gleaned intel suggesting two suppliers were at work, two rival drug smugglers, each eager to become the undisputed kingpin.

Mack Bolan had been waging a personal war on drugs for years. Just saying no was all well and good to teach young children, but the only certain method of stopping the vile spread was to eliminate the suppliers. So when Hal Brognola, his longtime friend and director of the Justice Department's Sensitive Operations Group, relayed the news that an informant had ratted out the exact date and location for a new shipment to arrive, the man known as the Executioner volunteered to stop the shipment from ever reaching the streets.

On a warm and muggy night, the soldier found himself flat on his belly on a low rise overlooking an isolated stretch of Louisiana shoreline. Garbed in a blacksuit and outfitted with the lethal tools of his specialized craft, he had been waiting for more than five hours for something to happen. A sliver of moon hung over the Gulf of Mexico, and from where he lay he could hear surf gently lap the beach.

A mosquito buzzed near Bolan's face, drawn by his body heat, but the insect repellant he had liberally used sent it winging off again. From the marsh to his rear came the croak of bullfrogs, the twitter of a bird and the high-pitched cries of young gators. Occasionally the deep roar of a full-grown male cowed everything else into temporary silence.

Now and then Bolan also heard rustling and slithery sounds from the high weeds that screened him. Snakes, he imagined, and hoped none were the poisonous varieties that called the marsh home.

To the soldier's right, perhaps fifty yards distant, glimmered a wide stream, one of dozens that flowed from deep within the bayou's recesses to empty into the Gulf. His gaze was focused on the mouth of the stream and the expanse of sea beyond.

According to the informant, ten million dollars' worth of cocaine was to be funneled inland before the night was done. Bolan meant to intercept the boat carrying it and have the vessel lead him to one of the two smugglers feuding over the lucrative trade, a particularly nasty piece of work who went by the name of Rabican. Whether that was his first or his last name, the Feds couldn't say. What they did know was that Rabican was a rogue Cajun who had a reputation for being as vicious as a rabid wolf. They suspected he was responsible for more than a dozen deaths in New Orleans and elsewhere.

Rabican's rival had a thicker file. Lafe Carbou had risen through the ranks to a position of eminence. He had been on the verge of becoming the single most powerful crime boss in the state when Rabican appeared on the scene, and in the short span of a year, built up an organization to rival Carbou's. The wily Carbou asked for a sit-down and proposed that Rabican come to work for him. The young upstart told him where he could stuff his offer, and the sit-down ended in a hail of lead that nearly claimed Carbou's life. Ever since, each man had done all in his power to eliminate the other. So far it was a draw, with Carbou in control of most major Louisiana cities and towns, and Rabican in control of most rural areas. A notable exception was Baton Rouge, Rabican's lone urban stronghold.

Bolan wanted them both shut down, permanently. Between them, they had smuggled in many millions of dollars' worth of cocaine and other drugs. Most of their illegal wares ended up in the hands of buyers in New York City, Chicago and San Francisco. Left unchecked, their operations threatened to spread to most of the Eastern Seaboard and the West Coast by year's end.

It had been hours since Bolan so much as twitched a muscle, a skill he had perfected as a sniper. But now he shifted slightly to relieve a cramp in his right leg. His forearms were draped across his M-16, his chin rested on his sleeve. As his eyes roved across the mouth of the stream for what had to be the hundredth time that night, he detected movement on the other side. Something large was at the water's edge. A deer, possibly, or even a bear.

The soldier raised the M-16 and molded his eye to the

Raptor night-vision scope. The thick vegetation across the stream came into stark green focus—and so did a tall figure dressed in camouflage fatigues and carrying a submachine gun.

Bolan's senses kicked into combat mode. He assumed the man had to be one of Rabican's goons, there to help escort the drug shipment inland. But the longer he watched, the more convinced he became there was more to the guy than met the eye. For one thing, the mystery man was rigged with military hardware, everything from an M-249 to body armor to a helmet. For another, the man had the unmistakable stamp of a soldier in the way he stood, the way he moved.

Bolan should know. He had been soldiering for decades and could tell another professional from an average joe at a glance. He wondered if it was possible the man was a Fed. DEA, maybe? Surely not. Brognola would have told him of any government operation in the area. Unless word hadn't trickled up through the chain of command.

From where Bolan lay, he could easily drop the mystery man with a single shot. But he dared not squeeze the trigger until he knew beyond all shadow of a doubt the soldier wasn't a friendly. Frowning, he watched as the man reached up and swung a single-tube night-vision goggle down over one eye. The small unit was attached to the man's helmet by a swivel.

The soldier scanned the Gulf several times, then shifted toward the heavy undergrowth from which he had emerged. Bolan saw his lips move. Someone else was there, someone hidden in the brush.

They had to be Feds, there to interdict the drugs. He debated making his presence known and decided against it. He had no identification with him. As far as the men across the stream were concerned, he would be regarded as a potential enemy and treated accordingly.

No, Bolan reasoned, the best course of action was to sit tight and see how events played out.

Suddenly a faint metallic purr wafted across the water, and the soldiers melted into the vegetation.

Bolan probed the Gulf with the scope. The purr grew to a dull growl, and far out on the water an approaching speck resolved itself into a low-slung speedboat. The craft was moving fast, aiming for the mouth of the stream. Bolan pegged it as an old Seahorse Mach II retrofitted with a top-end engine so it could outrun most any boat it encountered.

A hundred yards out, the helmsman throttled back, reducing speed by two-thirds.

He rose and surveyed the shoreline, apparently getting his bearings, and when he was sure, he piloted the speedboat into the stream.

Bolan expected the Feds to make their move, but no shots rang out, no hails of gunfire were directed at the craft. It cruised past the spot where he had seen the soldiers and was lost to view around a bend.

A heartbeat later a thicket parted. Out raced the man in question with three others, all similarly clad. They were lugging a large inflatable raft, complete with an outboard. Exhibiting military precision, they swiftly placed it in the water and climbed in. The outboard kicked over, and with the tall man at the rudder, the raft sped upstream after the speedboat.

Mystified, Bolan rose. If they truly were Feds, why had they let the drug runner slip by? Were they after bigger fish, the same as he was? The only way to find out was to follow them.

The soldier slung his M-16 and sprinted toward a wide

tract of high reeds where his own inflatable was concealed. It took only seconds to haul it into the open, climb in and head in pursuit.

His ramjet outboard motor had been modified for optimum performance with a minimum of noise. Even at full throttle it was as quiet as an idling car. The risk of being detected by the speedboat operator was next to nil.

The four men in the other raft were another story. They were using a ramjet, too, or an outboard motor a lot like it. Bolan never knew when they might take it into their heads to stop. In order not to blunder into them, he held to a slow speed and negotiated every bend with extreme caution. He always searched the next stretch before committing himself.

Mile after mile, veiled in darkness, the stream meandered steadily deeper into the wilderness. Bolan had consulted a map before beginning the op, but the map hadn't told him much other than that the stream ran generally northward, with a jag to the northwest about fifteen miles in. Several small tributaries fed into it at various points. The surrounding swampland was uninhabited. Quicksand, gators, water moccasins and mosquitos by the millions made the land a real-estate agent's nightmare.

In the dark the water was a dirty brown. The current was sluggish and posed no challenge to the outboard motor. Obstacles, though, were plentiful. Logs were common, many half-submerged. Bolan had to stay alert or suffer the consequences. In some places so much plant life choked the surface, it lent the illusion it was solid enough to walk on. Bolan had to be careful the prop didn't become entangled.

An additional obstacle had to be contended with from time to time—alligators. Only a few hundred yards in from the Gulf, Bolan negotiated a turn and saw what he thought was a large log directly ahead. He angled to the right to go around it when suddenly the log splashed to life and surged in the same direction. He narrowly averted a collision. Through the scope the alligator's eyes seemed to glow with preternatural light as it swam off.

Trees frequently hemmed the banks. Bolan had to duck under low limbs. Vines had to be pushed aside. Once when he reached for a trailing vine that dangled within inches of his face, the vine abruptly came alive, venting an angry hiss. He automatically grabbed for his knife, but the snake slithered up into the cypress.

Beyond the banks lay largely uncharted regions. The bows of adult gators intermixed with the croak of bullfrogs and a thousand and one other sounds. The marsh teemed with life. Most was harmful if not outright deadly to the few humans willing to brave its dangers.

To Bolan they were no more than mild distractions. He was at home in the wild. Much of his life had been spent in the hinterlands of the worlds, in thick jungles, in blistering deserts, in frozen tundra or on frigid alpine heights. He took what came in stride, with no more qualms than if he were walking down a city street. Yes, the wildlife posed a threat, but predictably so. Usually animals killed to fill their bellies or defend their territory. They rarely killed for the sheer sake of killing.

Humankind couldn't say the same. Bolan was a keen student of human nature, and it troubled him sometimes to contemplate that the human race was the most violent on the planet. Humans often killed out of simple savagery. The mugger who kicked a helpless victim to hear her bones break and the madman who unleashed an all-out war on a neighboring country were cut from the same sadistic cloth.

They were human, yet they were also less than human, and less than the beasts they were often compared to.

Bolan had come to the conclusion the only real monsters in the world were the two-legged variety. The only thing that held the monster in check was people like him.

Bolan liked to think of it as the War Everlasting. There would always be a place for warriors, for those willing to sacrifice their personal ambitions for the greater good. They were the flip side of the coin. For while they dispensed death, they killed only to save others. Their ideal was peace even if their methods were as violent as those they opposed.

The crack of a limb brought an end to Bolan's reverie. Something was on the west bank, something big. He swung around the M-16 and through the scope he glimpsed the rapidly retreating hairy hindquarters of a black bear.

Another mile went by. Bolan's every nerve was tense with raw anticipation. He had yet to catch sight of the other inflatable and hadn't heard the speedboat in a good long while.

More minutes dragged past, and on an impulse Bolan increased speed. His intuition was blaring. He should have caught a glimpse of the inflatable by now. Past the next turn lay a channel choked with lilies and water flowers. Bringing the raft to a stop, he studied the surface for sign the other two craft had gone through. The plants were undisturbed. There wasn't the slightest hint to suggest anyone was ahead of him.

"Damn," Bolan said under his breath and guided his inflatable into a tight U-turn. He had to pass close to the bank, and as he did, a startled raccoon chittered in indignation and bounded off.

The soldier remembered a tributary half a mile back, a

creek not much wider than his raft. He hadn't seen any evidence the other craft had taken it, but then again, he hadn't looked very hard. He had been acting on the assumption they would stick to the main stream.

Increasing speed, Bolan was cruising along a relatively open stretch of water when he spotted a pinpoint of light off to the northwest. He only had a glimpse. Distance was hard to gauge, but he guessed it was two miles.

The mouth of the creek was clear of obstructions. Bolan slowed and nosed the inflatable into the middle. The speedboat could have gone this way. There was enough room, but barely. Which might be deliberate.

By all accounts Rabican was a cunning SOB. He wouldn't make it easy for the Feds to find his widely scattered hideaways. A drug distribution point deep in the marsh, with access limited to a single narrow creek, was a masterful ploy. No one could approach without being detected. And Rabican was bound to have several avenues of escape inland, in case the Feds or his rival, Carbou, launched a full-scale strike.

High banks hemmed the creek, perfect for an ambush. They amplified the throb of the outboard motor, but Bolan didn't throttle down. Placing the M-16 across his lap, he made sure his Beretta 93-R was snug in its shoulder rig and his Desert Eagle secure in its holster on his hip.

The scope showed where the water lilies and other plants had been pushed aside by the passage of the speedboat and the other inflatable, leaving a clear belt of water in their wake. The creek twisted and turned, a further hindrance to penetration by hostile forces. Bolan had to watch out for snags and low limbs. He saw a snake glide off, and shortly thereafter, a big buck snorted and bolted.

Twice the soldier spied the light. Each time it was closer

but not close enough to reveal the source. By his best reck-
oning he was a mile and a half from the junction when he
rounded yet another bend and there, drawn up out of the
water onto the right bank, was the other raft. Instantly he
killed his outboard motor and veered to the left bank. When
the nose nudged solid ground, he hopped out and pulled
his raft into dense cover.

Forty yards ahead was another turn. A shadow among
shadows, Bolan prowled toward it. The four soldiers had
to be close by. And if they had stopped, it meant they
were close to the speedboat's destination. A sudden gust
of wind brought with it the sound of voices and gruff
laughter.

Bolan dropped into a crouch and crawled from tree to
tree, bush to bush. As he neared the bend, the creek
widened into a pond some thirty yards across. The light
reappeared. A lantern hung from a nail on a rickety dock
on the east bank, and tied to the dock was the speedboat.
Men were moving about, unloading the drugs. Bolan
counted seven through the scope. Three were doing the actual work, while two others were posted as sentries. The
last pair was talking.

Bolan was about to train the scope on where the drugs
were being taken when he realized he had seen one of the
talkers before. Or, to be more precise, the man's face. A
photo of it had been in Brognola's file.

It was Rabican himself.

There was no mistaking the high, sloping forehead, the
hawkish nose or the cruel cast to Rabican's hard features.
A cleft jaw and glittering dark eyes completed the picture.
He possessed a stocky build, thick shoulders and a bull
neck. In short, he looked exactly like what he was: a vicious thug. He wore casual clothes complemented by a pair

of pistols around his stout waist. The stub of a cigar was wedged between his lips but wasn't lit.

Rabican's presence was an unexpected bonus. Bolan had imagined it would take time to track the smuggler to his lair, but there he was, offered on a silver platter, as it were. The soldier had a clear shot, but shooting the dealer would alert Rabican's men and might imperil the federal agents.

Reluctantly Bolan eased his finger off the M-16's trigger. Sitting cross-legged with his back to a tree, he waited for the Feds to make their move. Tactically they should be fanning out to encircle Rabican's crew. They wouldn't open up until all four of them were in position.

Bolan wasn't an expert on ethnic characteristics, but he believed Rabican's men were mostly Cajuns. Their clothes, their accents, their manner of speech, laced with French idioms, were typical.

The cocaine was being unloaded from a secret compartment. Bolan saw a skinny Cajun heft a large bundle and step onto the dock. From there he moved toward a gap in the east bank. Beyond was a low hill or mound. Bolan figured the man would go up and over. Instead, the Cajun disappeared *into* the mound.

Bolan adjusted the scope for maximum gain and still couldn't make sense of what he had witnessed. He wondered if it might be a tent, but the scope revealed no trace of camouflage netting or tent struts. Then another Cajun emerged bearing a second lantern, and the combined light was enough to reveal Rabican's secret and confirm how devilishly devious the notorious smuggler truly was.

Louisiana's marshes were notorious for more than gators and bogs. Scattered throughout the region were underground formations known as salt mounds. Essentially great deposits of salt capped by large domes, they were also sources of natural gas, petroleum and sulfur. Some domes had been hollowed out, either by erosion or man-made means, and were used for storage.

Rabican was using a salt dome to secret the drug shipment. He had to use it regularly, Bolan deduced, then funnel the drugs to customers as needed. From the air no one would ever suspect. Even the rare fisherman or hunter who strayed this far into the marsh was unlikely to give the dome a second glance.

Soon the job was completed. Rabican was one of the last to file inside, taking the lantern from the dock with him. Inky gloom descended, alleviated by pale starlight and the sliver of moon. More than enough for Bolan's night-vision device to register movement across the way.

The Feds were converging on the dome.

Bolan liked how they used the lay of the land to best advantage, exercising stealth worthy of ninjas. The leader appeared to be a slim figure who directed the others by hand signals. They were almost to the dome when a man came ambling out toward the dock, his hands in his pockets, whistling softly to himself.

The four froze, and although the smuggler passed within a few yards of the slim leader, he never spotted them. As Bolan looked on, the slim one stalked the unsuspecting man, who walked to the end of the dock. A match flared, and the tip of a cigarette burned bright red. Puffs of smoke were blown skyward. The man gazed across the pond directly at Bolan without seeing him.

Through the scope Bolan watched the slim soldier slink up behind the nicotine addict. A thin arm flicked, encircling the man's head and yanking it back. A blade gleamed dully in the darkness. The man was dead before the knife stroke ended, slit from ear to ear. His head flopped to one side and his body swayed. Before it could pitch into the pond, two other camouflage-clad figures reached it, took hold of the arms and lowered it into the water with hardly a ripple.

An air-raid siren blared in Bolan's mind. Something was seriously wrong. Federal agents didn't go around slaying suspects without due cause. The quartet hadn't attempted to arrest the man or given him a chance to surrender. They had murdered him, plain and simple. A nagging suspicion began to eat at Bolan, a suspicion the quartet weren't agents, after all. Yet if that was the case, who were they?

The foursome were hastening toward the salt dome. Without hesitation they moved in. At any moment Bolan expected an outcry and the chatter of SMGs but nothing happened.

Rising, Bolan started around the pond. He had to find out who they were. With the stock of the M-16 tucked to his shoulder, he walked cautiously.

Security devices were absent. There were no cameras, no trip wires. Rabican relied on nature herself to discourage unwanted visitors.

Bolan was a dozen feet shy of the dock when he saw the body floating out toward the middle. The next moment a scaly reptilian form heaved up out of the depths and a razor-rimmed maw gaped wide. The alligator's jaws closed with a crunch, and with a mighty wrench it rolled completely over and was gone, taking its meal with it.

The entrance to the salt mound was mired in gloom. Two tunnels branched at right angles, both slanting underground. Bolan paused, debating which to take. A faint glow down the tunnel to the right decided the issue. With his back pressed to the rough, pitted wall, he crept lower.

The tunnel curved, the floor dropping by gradual degrees. Soon he spotted a lantern, suspended from a spike. Slinging the M-16, he drew his Beretta 93-R. From a pocket in his blacksuit he extracted a sound suppressor and threaded it onto the barrel A quick check of the magazine, and he was in motion again.

The tunnel curved sharply, preventing the soldier from seeing what was ahead. He heard voices but couldn't quite distinguish the words. Edging warily forward, he spied an opening in the left-hand wall. Light spilled through, and shadows flitted like moths. Loud laughter filled the tunnel.

Dropping into a combat crouch, the soldier moved to the opening and risked a peek. A spacious chamber had been carved from the salt. Stacked within were the bundles of cocaine unloaded from the speedboat, and they weren't the only bundles. Rabican had a cache any drug dealer in the country would drool over. Enough to keep the entire country in coke for the next decade. He also had crates of weapons, some opened, and a mountain of cardboard boxes that contained who knew what.

Rabican himself wasn't in the chamber but four of his flunkies were. They had finished unloading and were standing around awaiting orders. One was lighting a cigar.

Bolan edged backward and froze. A hard object had gouged him in the back of the head. He immediately recognized it as the muzzle of a gun.

The Executioner hadn't survived as long as he had by needlessly tempting fate. Whoever was behind him had only to squeeze the trigger and he was gator food. But if they'd wanted him dead, they could have shot him where he stood. Logically it was safe to assume they wanted him alive. Holding his arms out from his sides, he let the Beretta dangle from his forefinger.

A gloved hand relieved him of the machine pistol. He was gripped by the back of his nightsuit and pulled backward up the tunnel, the muzzle gouged against his head the entire time. He tried to turn his neck just enough to see his captor, but a sharp prod warned him not to.

Bolan was mildly surprised when he was ushered out of the dome and down the short path to the dock. His surprise grew when a question was whispered in his ear.

"Who the hell are you, mister? A Fed?"

Bolan didn't respond.

"Answer me, damn it. You're sure as hell not one of Rabican's dirtbags. Your getup, your gear, you must be with the DEA."

"I work with the Department of Justice," was as much as Bolan would reveal, and technically it wasn't a lie.

The man swore and spun him. It was the big soldier Bolan had seen earlier, his blue eyes mirror images of Bolan's own. His rugged features were pinched in agitation. "You pose a problem. I can't let her find you. There's no predicting what she'll do now that we've taken the plunge."

"She?" Bolan said quizzically.

The soldier put a finger to his lips and backed toward the undergrowth, beckoning for Bolan to follow.

Just then, from somewhere deep within the salt dome, came the crackle of an SMG. Pistols fired. Men shouted and screamed. The tall soldier gestured. "Hurry, damn it."

To say Bolan was confused was an understatement. He sensed the man had no intention of killing him and was, in fact, trying to save him from possible harm. Why that should be was beyond him. "Who are you people?"

"You saw us?" the soldier responded and swore. "If she finds out, she'll terminate you for sure. She won't want you reporting us. But I refuse to stoop to offing our own. You're only doing your duty."

"Isn't that what you're doing?"

The soldier gave him the most peculiar look. "There's no going back once you've crossed the line, friend," he said enigmatically. "I've made my bed, now I have to lie in it." Suddenly halting, he wagged the M-249. "On your knees, with your hands behind your head. Be quick about it."

There was a limit to how much Bolan would submit to.

He refused to let himself be knocked unconscious or handcuffed. So when the soldier slid around behind him, he tensed, coiling his legs.

Gunfire abruptly distributed the night, and five or six men spilled from the salt dome. They were firing as they backpedaled, pouring rounds into the tunnel in an effort to thwart pursuit. Among them, Bolan noticed, was Rabican.

"He's getting away!" Bolan's captor blurted as the smuggler and the gunners raced for the speedboat. "Stay where you are, mister! Don't interfere and you'll get out of this alive!" The man dashed toward the dock, cutting loose with the M-249.

Two of the hardmen fell, riddled like Swiss cheese. Rabican and the rest turned their attention on the soldier, who had dived prone.

Bolan had a decision to make. Heaving to his feet, he unslung his M-16. A gunner filled the scope and he stroked a quick burst that dropped the man in his tracks. Swiveling, he sought a new target, Rabican himself, but at the precise split second he fired, an underling blundered into his sights.

More triggermen emerged from the salt dome. Some were firing at whoever was after them. Others, at Rabican's command, opened up on the stand of vegetation in which Bolan was crouched. He had to eat dirt or take slugs. He ate dirt. Leaves and bits of tree limbs rained down, and the ground exploded in miniature geysers.

When Bolan glanced up, Rabican was in the speedboat, turning over the engine. His men jammed the dock, a few reloading, others firing wildly. Snaking to the right, Bolan sought a clear shot, but too many gunners were milling about. Rising, he darted behind a tree.

An explosion rocked the salt dome. Smoke spewed from

the entrance, and out of it, using the smoke as cover, rushed the soldier's three comrades. They unleashed a devastating firestorm that mowed down half the triggermen in the blink of an eye.

Bellowing commands, Rabican spun the wheel and opened the throttle to the max. The speedboat shot off across the pond toward the creek, and safety.

Like a Viking berserker of old, the slim leader of the strike squad charged into the midst of the gunners, downing them right and left. Bolan saw the figure clearly in his scope for the first time. A fatigue shirt and a Kevlar vest couldn't completely conceal the swell of an ample bosom, and loose-fitting fatigue pants didn't quite mask the shapely contours lower down. *It was a woman!* The "she" the soldier had referred to.

Her companions wiped out the last resistance. She pumped her arm twice, and in single file they sprinted south toward the creek. They hadn't gone ten feet when they were joined by the big soldier.

Bolan had to find out who they were. He broke into the open, and no sooner had he done so than two more of Rabican's flunkies barreled from the tunnel. They couldn't help but see him, and their reaction was predictable. They blistered the air with lead. One had a Remington revolver, the other an Uzi.

Bolan chopped them down with several rounds apiece. The delay cost him only a few seconds, but it was enough for the four unknowns to gain a substantial lead. He ran after them, and although he was in superb condition and could cover a hundred yards faster than most college track stars, they beat him to the creek, and their raft. When he reached the bend they were almost out of sight.

Bolan took another step, then stopped. He might be

able to catch them, he might not. He certainly couldn't overtake the speedboat. In his estimation it was better to let all of them go for now, and attend to the cache of drugs. Rabican was bound to radio his lieutenants and have a small army of gunners sent to transport the cocaine elsewhere before it was confiscated. Bolan couldn't allow that.

He lowed his M-16 and turned. He had enough C-4 to blow the dome sky-high.

He'd set it up to remote det, and once he had accomplished his primary mission, he would get on the horn to Hal Brognola and try to find answers to the questions uppermost in his mind: who were the four commandos? And what were they after?

Haversham Condominiums, Washington, D.C.

TIM CONSIDINE HAD ALWAYS wanted to be President of the United States. He loved the power that came with the position. Leader of the Free World. Chief Executive. Commander in chief. Being President was the next best thing to being God.

But Considine was honest enough to admit his dream would never come true. He loathed politics. He refused to compromise his ideals. And, perhaps most importantly of all, he had the charisma of a tree stump.

Early on, though, he had discovered he possessed a flair for clandestine strategy and tactics, and thanks to a father who had high connections in the State Department, upon graduation from Harvard he was accepted into the Central Intelligence Agency as an analyst. In the twelve years since, he had risen in standing to the exalted post of a deputy director for the ultrasecret National Intelligence Council.

To the public at large the NIC was just another bureaucratic department in an endless maze of government agencies and offices. To those in the know, however, the NIC was at the pinnacle of the intelligence community pyramid. Headed by a chairman and answerable only to the director of Central Intelligence, and through him to the President, the NIC played a crucial role in American's strategic planning.

Intel from all over the world was siphoned into the NIC's database. The information was analyzed by its cadre of experts, both in the public and private sectors, who then relayed their recommendations and insights up through the chain of command to the DCI and the President. Their role was all-inclusive. No global hot spot was overlooked. No situation was too big or too small.

When a high-ranking officer in a former Soviet republic went rogue and began selling high-tech weaponry on the black market, thereby threatening to destabilize much of Asia and the Middle East, the NIC proposed the tactical means of taking him down. When a chemical manufacturer was supplying banned chemicals to a despot for his biological weapons, the NIC supplied critical blueprints for stopping the flow.

Provided, of course, that Considine relayed the reports to his superiors and didn't take action on his own.

Considine was as loyal to his country as an American could be. His patriotism was beyond reproach. He staunchly believed in the fight against global evil, and in doing all he could to stop its spread. During his first ten years with the NIC, he had been content to perform his duties as required. Until the fateful day when it dawned on him that when all was said and done, he was nothing more than an exalted pencil pusher. An errand boy. A conduit for information others acted upon.

The NIC's role was strictly advisory. Glory boys in the DIA and the NSA and their ilk were handed the actual assignments. They were publicly praised for their efforts and rewarded with commendations and citations.

To Considine that was grossly unfair. He was lucky if he received an offhanded compliment from the chairman every now and again. Yet the job he did was every bit as important as the fieldwork performed by those various agency operatives. Even more so, in that they were acting on his recommendations based on the suggestions of the experts under him.

Considine was tired of being a pencil pusher. He wanted to get out in the field, to experience the thrill of espionage on the cutting edge. He had applied to agency after agency, and each one slapped him in the face. They had either offered him a position as an analyst or politely refused his field agent request on the grounds he lacked the proper training. One stuffed shirt went so far as to point out that his chances of passing the rigorous physical were slim to nonexistent.

So Considine glumly continued relaying intel and filing strategic updates. Then one morning he was reading The *New York Times* when he came across an account of how a company of Rangers had penetrated deep into Iraq to destroy a secret missile base impervious to air strikes. The Rangers were praised for their valor and fighting spirit, and the President had been commended for his daring in sending them in.

Considine read the article and bitterly laughed. If only the world knew! He was the one who submitted the recommendation to use the Rangers. The President had acted on *his* advice. If he'd had the authority, he could have sent in the Rangers himself and reaped all the glory and the accolades.

A fascinating new idea mushroomed. Considine sat at his kitchen table pondering a brainstorm so deliciously bold, he shuddered with excitement at the mere thought. What was to stop him from setting up his own little tactical unit for dealing with crises as he saw fit? The answer: nothing.

His first step had been to assemble a strike team. Since he enjoyed virtually unrestricted access to every government department and military branch, finding properly motivated candidates hadn't proved difficult. Especially when he deceived them into thinking their unit was officially sanctioned and so hush-hush they weren't to tell anyone.

Funding hadn't posed much of a problem. Much of it came from his unrestricted expense account. A few thousand here, a few thousand there. His travel expenses alone doubled, on paper at least, and no one took notice. And he had enough in personal savings to cover their "salaries." Equipment was another matter. He wasn't proud of how he had obtained most of it, but it had to be done.

Six months after Considine had his brainstorm, he had his strike team. It needed a proper designation, a code name, and after watching a show on the Discovery Channel about one of the most deadly creatures on the planet, he came up with the Scorpions.

For a year and a half all had gone well. Considine had sent his team on more than a dozen assignments. To Kazakhstan, to Pakistan, to Turkey, to Paris and elsewhere. They performed flawlessly, exceeding his expectations. But now something was dreadfully wrong.

Forgoing his breakfast, Considine grabbed his briefcase and hustled for the elevator. He was anxious to reach his office. It was imperative he contact the Scorpions and call them on the carpet. The way they were going, they would blow everything.

And he knew just who to blame.

HAL BROGNOLA LISTENED attentively to Mack Bolan's recital of the previous night's events, and when the soldier was done, the big Fed frankly admitted, "I don't have any idea who they were or what they were doing there. Your guess is as good as mine."

Bolan was phoning from a second-rate motel outside Baton Rouge. The connection was poor, and his normally deep voice came down the line tinny and broken. "That's just it. My original guess was wrong. Whoever they were, they sure as hell weren't DEA."

Brognola thoughtfully gazed out the window of his office in the Justice Department building. "It's a given they were after Rabican. The million-dollar question is, who sent them? I'll make some discreet inquiries at my end." The head Fed paused. "You're positive they were government and not just a hit squad sent by Carbou?"

"Positive," Bolan answered. "Unless Carbou somehow got his hands on some of the latest military gear."

"Do you still intend to stay down there until you've put both smugglers out of business?" Brognola inquired.

"Need you ask?"

The big Fed's mouth tweaked upward. "Just remember. There's a wild card in the mix now, and that always complicates matters."

"Tell me about it," Bolan said. "Your best bet might be the military angle. I'm willing to stake my bottom dollar the guy who pulled me out of there was a soldier."

"Could he have been a merc?"

Bolan went quiet. "My gut says no," he said at last. "He

could have killed me, but he didn't. A merc would have no such compunction."

"All right. Can I reach you at this number?"

"Leave a message at the desk and I'll get back to you. I have a lead on a local watering hole Rabican might frequent. I'm going there tonight to see what I can uncover."

"Stay frosty, Striker."

"Always."

The receiver filled with dial tone and Brognola hung up, the furrows in his forehead deepening. Making a tepee of his fingers, he bowed his chin to his chest and tried to make sense of the latest development. A four-person military strike team? With a female leader, no less. It seemed preposterous. The Defense Intelligence Agency had black ops units, but the threats they dealt with were global in nature. The Army, Marines, Air Force and Navy all had elite outfits, each with its own sphere of operations, ops that inevitably involved military threats to U.S. security.

A local smuggling war didn't qualify.

Brognola considered the Federal Bureau of Investigation, the Drug Enforcement Administration and the Justice Department itself. To his knowledge none was engaged in covert operations in Louisiana. The DEA was investigating Rabican and Carbou, but by the usual means. They wouldn't send in a hit squad. That wasn't how things were done. In America the rule of law reigned. The paranoid delusions of antigovernment types aside, most federal agents and soldiers abided by the laws they were sworn to uphold.

After a long and studied consideration, Brognola came to several conclusions. First, since he had complete faith in Bolan's judgment, the hit squad had to have military links. In which case they were rogues. And since he couldn't see a bunch of soldiers going around the country disposing of drug lords at random, they had to receive their orders from higher up. But from where? Or perhaps, more apt, from whom?

Sighing, Brognola picked up the phone again. He had a lot of calls to make. It was going to be a long night. But if someone was breaking every law on the books, he or she had to be stopped quickly.

LIKE EVERY CITY, Baton Rouge had its seamy side. No God-fearing citizen would be caught dead in certain quarters after dark.

The Strip, as it was called, was one of the seamiest ten blocks anywhere. Pimps, prostitutes and drug users roamed at will, outnumbering ten-to-one the few honest store owners and decent families too poor to leave.

On the corner of Belmont and Jasmine was a bar the police would dearly love to shut down. *Bayou Haven* blazed from its garish neon sign. At least once a week the cops were called to quell a disturbance or lock up a rowdy drunk. Muggings and knifings on the streets and alley adjoining it were so common that the area was known as the War Zone.

On this particular night, at half-past eleven, the Executioner came to the street corner across from the bar and stopped, waiting for the light to change. He was dressed in jeans, a bulky sweater and a dark blue windbreaker. A wool cap crowned his head. At a casual glance he'd pass for a longshoreman out for a night on the town.

Perfume tingled Bolan's nose, and around the liquor store to his left sashayed a lady of the night. A skintight red dress clung to her luscious hourglass body. She looked him up and down like a hungry wildcat sizing up prey, and jiggled her breasts in wanton invitation. "Hey there, handsome. Want some company?"

"No, thanks," Bolan said. The light changed and he started to cross.

The streetwalker glued herself to his elbow. "What's your rush, big man? The least you can do is hear me out."

"Only if it's in one word or less."

She didn't know how to take a hint. Playfully tugging on his arm, she said good-naturedly, "Come on. Pretty please? Be a sport. It's been a slow night, and I'm bored out of my skull."

Bolan looked at her, about to tell her to get lost. She wasn't much over twenty-one, if that, but her lifestyle was taking a toll. Her youthful beauty was prematurely fading. Crow's-feet lined her eyes, and her complexion was much too pale.

"Buy a girl a few rounds, why don't you?" she asked, nodding at Bayou Haven.

Three seedy characters were lounging outside the bar. Cajuns, judging by their speech and dialect. Telltale bulges under their jackets told Bolan they were armed. "Ever been in there before?" he asked.

Smiling broadly, the young woman nodded. "Dozens of times. I know all the bartenders by their first names."

"A few rounds it is, but nothing more."

"Well, this is a switch," she bantered. "Usually men can't keep their paws off me long enough for me to finish my first drink. Let me guess. You're a monk in disguise?"

Bolan grinned and shook his head. "I'm here on business, not for pleasure."

"What kind of business?" the woman asked, examining him more closely. "Hey, you're not a cop, are you? I don't want anything to do with you if you are. They don't take kindly to the law in there."

"I'm not a police officer," Bolan assured her. "I'm looking for someone." The Cajuns didn't give him a second glance as he opened the door for her.

The woman smiled at one of the men and said, *"Bonsoir,* Dayka. What be happening?"

Dayka's dark eyes flicked to Bolan and back to her. "What were you doing last week, Nina? We missed you."

"I had a live one," Nina said, and winked.

The place was almost packed. Distinctly Cajun music, heavy on the fiddle, blared from two speakers high on the walls. Bolan took Nina's hand and steered her toward an empty corner table. No one paid any attention, which he construed as a good sign.

Bolan sat with his back to the paneled wall and folded his hands in front of him. He caught snatches of conversation, but trying to make sense of it was like trying to decipher a code. A lot was in French, mixed with Cajun expressions and dialect. Words that were like Greek to him.

Nina had placed her small purse on the table. "So, who is it you're looking for? Maybe I can help."

"An acquaintance." Bolan would rather she didn't know. She was on friendly terms with the Cajuns, some of whom might have ties to Rabican. The previous night, as he roamed the salt dome setting charges of C-4, he had come across a pack of matches. On the cover was the name and address of Bayou Haven. As leads went, it wasn't a strong one, but he would take what he could get.

"This person have a name?"

"Did you come here for a drink or to pester me?" Bolan rejoined, smiling to demonstrate he wasn't angry at her.

Nina chuckled and swiped a hand at her bangs. "Touché. I can be too curious for my own good. One time I asked a john so many questions about his personal life, he got mad and slugged me senseless."

Bolan was scanning the patrons without being obvious. It was a long shot, expecting Rabican to be there. A lusty whoop from the dance floor drew his gaze to an older couple dancing with extraordinary zeal. Onlookers were cheering them on. Everyone was friendly and in good spirits.

"Fine folks, these Cajuns," Nina said, staring fondly in the same direction. "They'll give you the shirts off their back if you earn their trust."

The three men who had been outside materialized out of the crowd, moving toward their table. The one she had called Dayka was in the forefront. Tall and muscular, he had an air of self-assurance.

"Here comes your buddies," Bolan mentioned.

Nina glanced over her shoulder. "Dayka and I share drinks on occasion but I don't know the other two. I see them here from time to time, though. Word is, they can get you any kind of drug you want, any time."

Bolan's interest in the pair perked. They were typical hardcases; cold eyes, cold expressions fixed intently on him.

"What's up, Dayka?" Nina said as the three men came to a stop.

"Your friend here," the tall Cajun said, nodding at Bolan. "We think maybe we take him out in the alley and have a little talk with him."

The other two men slipped their hands under their jackets.

3

Tim Considine was cautious when he left his condo at midnight. He drove slowly and checked the rearview mirror every few seconds to ensure he wasn't being tailed. When he reached the restaurant on Forester Avenue, he circled the block three times before he wheeled into a parking space.

The others were already waiting in a booth by a corner window. Two other customers were at the counter, and that was it. The restaurant was open twenty-four hours, but after eleven p.m. business was slow.

Considine smiled at the waitress. She had waited on him before and always treated him nicely. His smile faded as he approached the table, and he adopted his most severe expression. "I'm glad all of you could make it," he said testily as he slid into the booth.

"What choice did we have?" Madeline Culver responded. She was as thin as a whip but as strong as most men. Considine has chosen her because she had been at the top of her class at the police academy until she was caught cheating on an exam and drummed out despite her repeated denials of wrongdoing. "You told us to be here or else we'd regret it."

"I don't like being threatened," said the black-haired man beside her. Rico Fuentes had been in the Marine Corps. While serving embassy duty in Greece he had been involved in an unfortunate incident involving a diplomat's daughter. He had literally been caught with his pants down while on duty, and his military career had come to an abrupt end.

The big man on Culver's left was Kyle Carson. A former Ranger, a member of the elite First Battalion, Seventy-fifth Regiment, his mistake had been costliest of all. He had been overseeing a routine training exercise involving parachute drops, and two recruits had died when their chutes became entangled on the way down. Carson had done everything by the book. But technically, he had been in charge, and worse, one of the recruits was the son of a two-star general who wasn't the forgiving type.

That left the fourth member of Considine's strike force. George Placer had been a crack DEA agent, but some drugs turned up missing from a drug bust he headed. Blame was placed on his shoulders, and although Placer denied it vehemently and fought his dismissal in court, he found himself out of a job and blacklisted.

Considine stared from one to the other, then said with deliberate sarcasm, "My Scorpions, I selected you. I picked you from a list of over a hundred candidates to become the best of the best. America's ultimate line of defense against the vermin of this world. And this is how you repay me?"

No one said a word. Carson averted his eyes. Culver's jaw clenched.

"The Scorpions are *my* brainchild," Considine stressed. "I gave each of you a chance to redeem yourselves in the eyes of your country. I've gone to incredible lengths on your behalf. And this is how you repay me?" he repeated angrily.

"Don't blow a gasket," Culver said.

"And don't you tell me what to do, Maddy," Considine shot back.

Carson cleared his throat. "How did you find out, sir?"

"Did you think I wouldn't?" Considine retorted, leaning forward. "I'm privy to every piece of intel gathered by every U.S. agency from the CIA to the Coast Guard. That business with the card in Paris had me wondering. I had forbidden Maddy to do it again, but the very next mission she left another of her calling cards in the mouth of that heroin transporter in Izmir, Turkey."

"There was a method to my madness," Culver said, smirking.

Considine's blood was boiling. "Little did I realize—" He stopped and straightened and put on another warm smile for the approaching waitress, although he didn't feel like smiling. He felt like ripping out Culver's throat.

"What will it be?" the pretty waitress asked. "The special tonight is pie à la mode. Pecan pie with vanilla ice cream."

"Coffee will do just fine," Considine said.

"Can I get any of you refills?" she asked the others as she filled his cup. Only Fuentes accepted.

A strained silence lasted until she was gone. Then Considine started right in again.

"Little did I realize you had plans to go into business

for yourselves. I have it on reliable authority you're offering your services to anyone who can meet your price."

"Four hundred thousand per job," Culver said proudly. "Split four ways. Our latest is a lowlife drug dealer. He slipped through our fingers last night, but we'll nail his sorry ass soon enough."

Considine sat back, stunned at how casually she had flung it in his face. "How could you?" His sense of personal hurt was exceeded only by an acute feeling of betrayal. "After all I did for you? After I gave each of you a chance to start over with a clean slate?"

"Spare us the speech," the woman said. "Sure you did us a favor, but what did we get out of it?"

"The satisfaction of knowing you've helped your country. You have done America proud, and you should be proud yourselves. Few others could do what you've done," Considine said, reciting his litany. "Everyone from the President on down is grateful."

"So you keep saying," Culver said. "But the President has never thanked us, has he? So I repeat, what the hell do we get out of working for you except the privilege of having our heads blown off?"

"Patriotism is its own reward. Duty well done is payment enough." Considine had given them the same pitch when he signed them on. It had worked wonderfully then. Now their outlook had changed. Culver was to blame. She had always been too independent, but he never expected her to go so far astray. Not that he didn't have a contingency prepared, anyway.

"Oh, please," Culver answered in mild disgust. "You're not putting your life on the line day in and day out." Lowering her voice, she gasped, "God and country don't put nice clothes on my back or a Jag in my garage. We'll still do jobs for you, but we'll continue to freelance as we see fit. If all goes well, in a couple of years we'll be able to retire and live like kings."

"Is money all that matters?" Considine challenged, and only Carson displayed any guilt.

"You haven't been listening," Culver said. "We'll go on working for you, but on our terms, not yours."

"That's totally unacceptable." Considine mechanically raised his coffee cup but set it back down without taking a sip. "You are to cease and desist with your personal activities. Failure to comply will result in your termination and replacement."

"Was that a threat?" Culver wanted to know.

"Take it any way you want." Considine was through being reasonable. They had perverted the noble purpose he set for them, taken his dream and flung it in his face. He would love to see them hauled up on charges. But he couldn't. Because, by rights, the Scorpions were an outlaw unit with no official sanction. If he reported them, they would tell everything, and he would be arrested, too. His career would be ruined. He might end up spending the rest of his life behind bars.

The Scorpion leader was staring at him as if he were a fly she yearned to swat. She tapped the table several times.

"I'll be back in a minute," Fuentes said, sliding out. "Nature calls." He ambled off.

Considine decided to try bluffing them into bowing to his will. "All I have to do is pick up a phone and within the hour all four of you will be in custody. Is that what you want?"

"You wouldn't dare," Culver snapped. "As you keep reminding us, the Scorpions are your baby. If we go down in flames, so will you. You'll be called on the carpet for letting us get out of control. Is that what you want?" she mimicked him.

"Try me and find out," Considine said, then threw them a carrot. "Look, if you stop now, before it's too late, I'm willing to overlook your indiscretions and get on with business as usual. Each of you go home. Think about it. I'll contact you by the end of the week, and we'll have another sit-down."

Culver surprised him by slowly nodding. "Maybe you're right, sir. Maybe we should reconsider our options."

"Sure," Placer said. "It would be insane to take on the entire United States government."

"Now you're being sensible." Considine smiled and consulted his wristwatch. It was past one, and he had to be up by six. "I have to go. Consider everything I've said, and you'll realize it's in your own best interests." Polishing off the rest of his coffee, he rose. "I hope there are no hard feelings."

"None at all," Culver said.

Carson wouldn't look up, which Considine construed as a sign the former Ranger did indeed hold it against him. How ironic. He had rated Carson as the most dependable, as the most dedicated to the cause. "Fill in Rico when he gets back," he instructed them, and headed for the cash register to pay. The pretty young waitress accepted his money, and he told her to keep the change.

Considine hadn't bothered to lock his car. He climbed in, inserted his key into the ignition and within moments was wheeling onto Forester Avenue.

BOLAN COULDN'T SAY exactly what had gone wrong. Maybe it was the fact he wasn't Cajun. Maybe the locals were suspicious of strangers. Or maybe Dayka regarded him as dangerous. Some people had a sixth sense whenever they met a wolf in human guise. He should know. His own intuition had served him well in that regard many times.

Trash cans and discarded boxes cluttered the alley. The instant the door closed, Dayka placed a hand against Bolan's chest and pushed him against the wall. "Now let's see who you are, eh?" His other hand delved into the pockets of Bolan's zipped-up windbreaker.

The soldier knew the Cajun wouldn't find a wallet or a driver's license or any other form of identification. He had left it in his rental car. "You have no right to do this," he said, playing the part of an indignant victim. "Tell me what this is all about, or so help me I'll have the police down on your heads."

"We think maybe you're not what you seem to be," Dayka said. He had only two more pockets to go. "So be a good boy or maybe we take you for a ride in the country."

Bolan wasn't going anywhere. He waited until Dayka's hand slipped into his last pocket, then exploded into motion. A solid uppercut to the tip of Dayka's jaw rocked the Cajun's head back and Bolan thrust his hand higher, raking it across Dayka's face. The man staggered, blood spurting, dazed but not out.

The Executioner sprang past him. The other two were a shade slower in unlimbering their hardware, and paid for it. Bolan's foot caught one in the groin, doubling the man in over. Whipping into a spin kick, he connected with the last Cajun's cheek, slamming the man into a cluster of trash cans. The cans and the Cajun crashed to the ground with a tremendous racket.

Pivoting, Bolan planted his foot in the face of the man who was doubled over. It catapulted the hardman into the wall, and there was a loud crunch. Dayka was still on his feet, but he was weaving drunkenly while trying to jerk a revolver from under his belt. Another uppercut rocked him onto his heels. A right cross dropped him in his tracks.

That left the Cajun scrabbling up out of the trash cans. His hand flashed out from under his jacket, but he wasn't holding a gun. He had a fancy double-edged dagger, and he seemed to be adept at using it. He came in low and fast, slashing right and left.

Bolan retreated, dodging and twisting to evade the blade. He had a knife of his own up his left sleeve, and his Beretta in its shoulder harness, but he didn't want to kill the guy if he could help it. A body would bring the police and create too much commotion. Rabican would never show. So rather than kill his attacker, when the Cajun made the mistake of overextending himself, Bolan settled for lunging, grabbing the man's wrist and locking his elbow with a sharp twist. Driving his right knee up and in, Bolan was rewarded with the crack of bone. The Cajun's dagger skittered to the pavement, and the man threw back his head to screech in agony, a shriek Bolan nipped in the bud with a punch that folded him like an accordion.

Bolan stepped back, surveying his handiwork. The trio would be out for a while. Adjusting his jacket and cap, he calmly reentered the bar.

Nina was sipping a vodka gimlet. She beamed as he slid into his chair and clutched his wrist. "Hey, you're back! That was quick. Dayka and his friends weren't too rough on you, were they?"

"Not at all," Bolan said.

"Cajuns don't take to outsiders much," Nina mentioned. "They tend to stick to their own affairs, and I can't say I blame them. The police are always nosing around. Sniffing for drugs, most likely."

Bolan took advantage of the opportunity. "Are drugs dealt here?"

"Hell, no. Do these people look like druggies to you?" Nina laughed at the notion. "They don't go in for that crap. Give them a keg and a roast pig and they're as happy as larks." She leaned across the table. "I've heard rumors, though. One of them has gone bad in a big way. He's into the hard stuff. As a seller, not a user."

"Ever seen the guy?" Bolan asked, trying not to sound too interested.

"Someone pointed him out to me once, months ago. He comes here fairly often but always keeps to himself. Him, and that gorgeous babe of his."

"A girlfriend?"

"So they say. Belle is her name, and there isn't a man alive who wouldn't give his right arm to be in Rabican's shoes."

"Rabican?" Bolan feigned ignorance.

"The fellow I was telling you about. Someone you don't want to mess with. They say he buries bodies in the bayou as often as a farmer plants seeds." Nina shuddered. "I want nothing to do with him or his men. So don't you go repeating what I've told you. I'll deny every word."

"Don't worry," Bolan said. It was the confirmation he needed. Now all he had to do was wait. But not there. Dayka and the others wouldn't be unconscious for long. He ordered a drink but hardly touched it, and after five more minutes elapsed, he stood up. "I have to be going. Nice meeting you."

Nina's disappointment was sincere. "So soon? I was looking forward to spending some time together. You're a quiet one, and I like that in a man. Most talk my ears off with lies about how much money they earn and what big shots they are."

"Sorry," Bolan said, touching her cheek. "I have to get to work."

"The night shift, huh?" Nina said, and rather sadly scanned the patrons. "I guess that makes two of us. Thanks, mister, for being so sweet."

Bolan had been called a lot of things in his time but sweet wasn't one of them. He shouldered through the boisterous crowd, out into the cool night air. Crossing Belmont, he stood in deep shadow in the recessed doorway to a clothing store. No one could see him, but he could see everyone who came and left Bayou Haven.

Time dragged, but Bolan was a patient man.

A sign in the bar had let Bolan know it closed at two a.m. By one-thirty he was about convinced Rabican wouldn't appear. A few minutes later, a white stretch limousine pulled up to the curb. Bolan straightened, but it disgorged two slabs of muscle, not his quarry. They strutted inside as if they owned the place. He gave them no more thought until they suddenly reappeared.

They weren't alone. Dayka was with them, a towel pressed to his ravaged face. And between the two newcomers, held in an iron grip, was an extremely scared Nina. She struggled, but they shoved her into the back seat and piled in after her.

Bolan's gut balled into a knot. She was in trouble and it was his fault. The limo pulled out, driving right past. Tinted windows prevented him from seeing inside. At the corner it turned right.

Putting on a burst of speed, Bolan ran for his rental car, a dark brown Taurus. He had parked it around the block, and he feared the limo would be long gone by the time he turned onto Magnolia. But there it was, five blocks ahead, driving slightly under the speed limit. The hardmen weren't taking a chance of being stopped.

Bolan stayed well back. He let other vehicles pass him to reduce the odds of being spotted. The limo turned onto Brouissard Avenue, bearing west. He suspected they were making for Interstate 10, and he was right. Once they were across the Mississippi River and in West Baton Rouge, they held to fifty-five miles per hour.

A road atlas was in the glove compartment. So was a pencil flashlight. Laying the atlas on the seat beside him, Bolan flicked on the beam and flipped to the map of Louisiana. Rimming the page were inserts of every major city, including Baton Rouge. He saw that the interstate curved to the southwest, toward largely uninhabited swampland.

After about fourteen miles an exit sign appeared. They were nearing State Highway 77. The limo's turn signal came on, but Bolan left his off. He didn't want the blinking light to attract the limo driver's attention. Going off the interstate, he slowed to ten miles per hour. By the time he came to a stop sign, the limo had turned south and was a quarter of a mile ahead.

Traffic was sparse. Rural folk didn't keep late hours. The farther south they traveled, the fewer farmhouses and isolated homesteads they saw.

The limousine's taillights were the size of fireflies. But Bolan was confident he wouldn't lose them. The farmland was slowly being replaced by swampland. Through his open window wafted the familiar croak of bullfrogs and the booming bows of alligators. A moth as big as a sparrow hit his windshield with a loud splat. An opossum darted across the asphalt up head, young clinging to its side.

The limo turned again, onto a dirt road winding off into nowhere. The dust it raised shimmered in the starlight.

Switching off his headlights, Bolan braked. His was the

only other vehicle on the road. If the limo's occupants spotted it, they might wonder what another car was doing there so late. Only after their taillights disappeared did he press on the gas. He left his headlights off.

Driving without lights was a tricky proposition. It was hard to tell exactly where the edge of the road ended and the swampland began. At any moment a deer or some other large animal might bolt into his path, but the soldier doggedly pressed on.

The limo turned again, heading north.

At the junction Bolan stuck to the middle. The next stretch was narrow and hemmed by thick growth alternated by patches of water that gave off a dank smell laced with other odors. A few were pleasant, most were much less so. Every so often large forms that looked like logs but moved under their own power swam off as his car approached them.

Bolan hoped Nina wouldn't come to harm before he caught up. Her abduction was unexpected. The men at the bar knew her. She as a regular. They had no reason to suspect she was linked to him other than that they arrived together. But to her, he had just been another john. Perhaps they only wanted to question her. Yet if that were the case, why had they hauled her off into the boondocks? She was in danger, and he was to blame. Come what may, he had to help.

It wasn't in Bolan's nature to sit by and do nothing while an innocent suffered. Some people could. He remembered reading a newspaper account of a woman who was stabbed more than dozen times and raped. She screamed for help while she was being attacked, and forty-one people heard her. But no one came to her aid. They shut their windows or plugged their ears or turned up the volumes on their televisions and stereos. And she died.

To Bolan, those people were as much to blame as the rapist. Their inaction resulted in a heinous crime that could have been prevented. Proving, yet again, that apathy was evil in itself.

Bolan had never shared that attitude. When he saw someone in misery, he had an instinctive urge to alleviate their suffering. To help. To make a difference. And he did it the best way he knew how. He wasn't a surgeon with the skill to save countless lives on an operating table. He wasn't a minister with the selfless faith to heal the human soul. He was a warrior. He fought evil on its own terms. On the most basic of levels. An eye for an eye and a tooth for a tooth. And he made no apologies to anyone.

Several lights appeared in the distance.

Some sort of compound was a mile up ahead. He looked for a spot to pull over, but the swamp came right up to the road's borders. Halfway there he decided to stop where he was. Then he spotted a spur of solid ground on the right. It wasn't much wider or longer than the car, but it sufficed. Killing the engine, he climbed out and walked around to the trunk. Inside was his duffel bag with an assortment of weapons.

Bolan chose his old reliables—his Desert Eagle, the M-16, an extra Beretta 93-R and a couple of grenades.

He wanted to change into his blacksuit but every second counted. There was no telling what Rabican's men were doing to Nina. He shoved spare magazines for the rifle and both pistols into his pockets, and was ready.

At a quick jog, Bolan made for the compound. He could sustain the pace for hours. He stopped once, briefly, to train the Raptor Scope on the site and mark the location of several corrugated tin buildings. They were protected by a perimeter fence crowned by strands of barbed wire. Spotlights were positioned at regular intervals. The limousine, a Jeep and a sedan were parked inside the fence in a small parking area. No one was moving, but there were bound to be guards.

Lowering the M-16, Bolan jogged on, his soles slapping the ground in a steady cadence. In the swamp to his right something submerged with a loud splash. Out of the strip of woodland to his left came the bleat of a doe or a fawn. He was less than two hundred yards from the fence when a thicket rustled, and from it bounded a four-legged creature that planted itself in his path, growled deep in its throat and bared gleaming fangs.

4

Tim Considine switched on his car radio to listen to the all-news station. It was the only station he listened to. He tried to concentrate on the national news but couldn't. Too much was at stake. His dream. His career. His future. Where had it all gone so wrong?

Considine supposed his big mistake was in thinking he could rehabilitate someone like Madeline Culver. He was positive she was the instigator. Without her to egg them on, the others would never have stepped out on their own. Yet she had fit the candidate profile he developed perfectly. She was innocent of the charge against her—or so he had presumed—and eager for a second chance. Only now did he realize she had to have been guilty all along. The same with Placer and maybe Fuentes. But not Kyle Carson. Carson was too much the soldier, too devoted to his country.

All the way to his condo Considine mulled the issue of

what to do should they refuse to agree to his terms. He had reached a decision by the time he pulled into his usual parking space. Even if Culver and the others repented, he could never trust them fully again. Drastic action was called for. He had to terminate his first team. The thought saddened him immensely. He had gone to so much effort, taken so many risks. And for a while there they had performed superbly. It was a shame they hadn't worked out.

But that was what his contingency plan was for.

His dream wasn't at fault, Considine reflected, as he hurried up the sidewalk. The problem lay in those he had picked to carry out the dream. They had proved unworthy. He needed to start over again with a whole new squad. And next time, he'd pick people whose patriotism was beyond reproach.

Everyone made mistakes. The important thing was to learn from them and to take steps to keep them from recurring. With a little extra work, Considine could rebuild the Scorpions into a better unit. A unit that wouldn't go astray. A unit that would obey him to the letter.

The doorman was coming to open the door for him. Considine checked his watch, wishing the old man would move faster. A sound caused him to turn. He thought he'd heard a car door quietly close. A check of the parking lot revealed it had to have been his imagination.

"Good evening, Mr. Considine," the doorman greeted him. "You're out late."

"It's been one of those days, Fred," Considine said. He slipped past the man to the elevators.

"What were you looking at out there?" Fred asked.

"I thought I heard a noise, but it was nothing." The NIC man pressed the button to go up, and the elevator door pinged open.

"Really? I'll go check. We've had a problem with kids keying cars." Fred palmed his flashlight.

"You do that," Considine said, amused by the mental image of the old man trying to catch a gang of teenagers. The elevator door closed, and he punched the button for his floor. Once in his condo he went straight to the special phone by his bed and made the recording that would set the wheels of retribution in motion. Then he indulged in his nightly ritual. He undressed and hung his suit on a hangar. He aligned his shoes in their proper position at the bottom of his closet. He put on pajamas, brushed his teeth, flossed and gargled with mouthwash. Switching out the lights, he climbed into bed and laid back on his fluffy pillow with a sigh.

Considine closed his eyes and tried to drift to sleep, but his mind was racing faster than a jet aircraft. He couldn't stop thinking of the Scorpions, his Scorpions, and how it had all gone wrong. How silly of Culver to think he wouldn't hear about those calling cards she had started sticking into the mouths of their assigned targets. The very first time, with Perigord in Paris, he had demanded to know why, and she had grinned ever-so-sweetly and said she thought it was a nice touch. "Our trademark," she had called it, "so everyone will know it was us."

Appalled by her stupidity, Considine has pointed out the Scorpions were a clandestine operation. No one was supposed to know they existed. He had reprimanded her severely, and she had apologized. But he saw now she had only been stringing him along. She kept leaving the cards. Her purpose was to get the word out to people in the intelligence community and the underworld. That way, when she contacted potential clients, the calling cards the team had left became their résumé.

Damned ingenious, Considine had to admit. He wondered how she selected her clients, and it occurred to him she had to be using the list of probable targets he worked up each month. Culled from the worldwide wealth of intel the NIC was privy to, the list usually contained fifteen to twenty names of individuals the world would be better off without. After considering logistics and expenses, he always whittled it down to just one. He didn't deem it wise to have the Scorpions hit more than a single target a month.

Considine should have realized something was up even before he heard about the calling cards. Culver had always shown an exceptional interest in the monthly lists. He'd chalked it up to enthusiasm but in reality she had been using him. The longer he thought about it, the angrier he became. He couldn't wait to replace her—

What was that?

Considine opened his eyes and sat up. He could swear there had been a faint noise in the living room. He listened, and when it wasn't repeated, he laid back down. No one could break in without alerting him. Not only were there triple locks on the door, he had an electronic security system second to none. It would take someone with highly specialized training to slip in undetected.

The thought of training angered Considine even more. He had gone to incredible lengths to work up phony credentials and authorizations to get his team into regularly conducted training sessions offered by various law-enforcement agencies and the military. It hadn't been easy, but he wanted them to be the best. Every tactical aspect had been covered, from sniping to demolition to surveillance. He even had them take a course in surreptitious entry, as the CIA dubbed it, which covered how to break into secure buildings and—

Considine's eyes snapped open again, and he sat up with a start. Fear spiked through him, but he suppressed it. Out of the corner of an eye he registered movement and started to turn. He told himself it couldn't be, he had to be wrong, they wouldn't dare. Then a jarring blow to the temple knocked him flat. There was surprisingly little pain. An image floated before him, a face he recognized. It was smirking.

A dark veil closed over him, and Considine wondered if this was how it felt to die.

THE EXECUTIONER MOLDED the eyepiece to his right eye. Revealed in the garish glare of the lens was a large German shepherd. A guard dog, evidently left to roam outside the gate rather than inside. And it was well-trained. Venting a feral snarl, the dog launched itself at him like a fur-covered comet. He had no recourse but to stroke the M-16's trigger. The rifle fired three times, and the dog crumpled in a twitching heap.

Bolan scoured the vicinity for the shepherd's handler, but no one was anywhere near. Puzzled, and doubly cautious, he walked to within a stone's throw of the chain-link fence. The gate was closed and padlocked. No Trespassing signs were posted every twenty-five feet. On the nearest tin building, painted in large block letters, was a large sign that proclaimed Canbiar Landscaping, Incorporated.

The name was an anagram. Bolan unscrambled the letters *CANBIAR* and grinned. Rabican probably thought he was being clever, but he couldn't be any more obvious if he tried.

As yet there was still no sign of guards. Bolan angled off the road, moving to the left along the base of the fence. He saw no cameras, no sensors. He did find a hole in the bottom of the chain-link fence, though. Two feet across and a foot high, it explained how the guard dog had slipped out.

Flattening, Bolan looked both ways, then crawled through. No sirens blared. No shouts were raised. The compound was as peaceful as a library.

Shadows cloaked Bolan as he moved to the rear of the first building, and on around the rear to the opposite corner. He put an ear to the tin but heard no sounds from within. If not for the vehicles, he would swear the place was deserted.

Suddenly a door in the next building opened, and out sauntered two men in flannel shirts and overalls. They looked the part of landscapers, but the Uzis they were toting proved otherwise. Their dialects revealed them to be Cajuns, and other than a few words here and there, Bolan had no idea what they were talking about. They walked toward the front of the compound and commenced a sweep of the fence.

The moment they were out of sight, Bolan sprinted to the second building. Twisting the brass doorknob, he put an eye to the crack. A dimly lit hall led left, past a couple of closed doors to another door partway open. Voices reached him. So did the sound of a slap. Slinging the M-16, Bolan drew his Beretta. In a crouch, he sidled to where he could see into the room.

Nina was lashed to a chair. Blood was trickling from a corner of her mouth, and she had a nasty welt on her cheek. Pacing back and forth in front of her, his back to the doorway, was Dayka.

"What was that man doing at Bayou Haven, girl?"

Tears welled from Nina's eyes. "How many times must I tell you? I never set eyes on him before tonight. I don't know who he was or what he was up to."

Dayka slapped her again, and she sagged and groaned. "Don't lie," he warned, "or you be dead before the night is done."

Bolan crept closer. He had to know if any others were inside before he committed himself.

"Honest to God," Nina said, weeping, "if I knew anything, I'd tell you." She looked up. "I thought we were friends, Dayka. How can you do this to me?"

"Two friends are in the hospital because of that guy, and me, I have the mother of all headaches. He's no ordinary man. He fights like he was born to it. Like someone who does it a lot. Now where he learn to beat three men with his bare hands, you suppose?"

"How would I know?" Nina responded and was hit so hard the front legs of her chair left the floor. She sagged again, barely conscious.

Entwining his fingers in her hair, Dayka jerked her head up. "I don't like doing this. Make it easy or I be rougher. Orders are orders."

Elsewhere in the room someone swore. "Quit the nice and do her right. T. Boy and me don't want to be here all damn night."

"I don't think she knows a thing, Mazoo," Dayka said.

"Rabican says to be sure," Mazoo responded. "Use your knife and carve her. If that doesn't loosen her tongue, nothing will."

The third man spoke. "Give her to me for half an hour, and she'll give us her life's story. I guarantee."

Dayka shook his head. "You like the blood too much, T. Boy. This one be a friend of mine. I'd rather she not suffer so much." He shook Nina by the chin. Her eyelids fluttered but didn't open.

"You getting soft, Dayka," T. Boy said. "I remember when you gutted your own cousin and grinned doing it."

"My cousin was a bastard." Dayka reached under his jacket. A switchblade flashed, and he pressed the sharp edge to the woman's cheek. "As soon as she wakes up, I'll start with the face. Women don't like having their faces cut. They're scared of being ugly."

Bolan had their positions fairly well pegged. Taking another step, he kicked the door inward.

T. Boy was one of the men who had taken Nina from the bar. He was lounging against the far wall, his arms folded. He wore a shoulder holster and stabbed for his FEG PMK-380, but a slug from Bolan's Beretta ensured he never touched it.

Mazoo was T. Boy's partner. He was in a reversed chair, his arm hanging over the back. He had a Browning Hi-Power. But to draw it he had to reach around the chair and the split-second delay was costly. As the Beretta fired, Mazoo and his chair pitched to the floor.

Dayka was no fool. He didn't attack. He leaped behind Nina, jerked her chin high and pressed his knife to her throat, drawing blood. "Drop the gun, or I slit her neck!"

Bolan had a clear shot. A twitch of his finger, and it would be over. But there was always the chance Dayka's knife would slice into Nina as he fell, opening her jugular. Bolan lowered his pistol.

"I said drop it! And lose the rifle."

The Cajun was scared, and scared men did irrational things. Bolan relaxed his fingers, and the 93-R thumped at his feet. He unslung the M-16 and let it slide to the floor. "Let the girl go. She was telling the truth."

"You came all this way to save a woman you hardly know, is that it?" Dayka said sarcastically. "I be what kind of fool, you think?"

Bolan had to take the Cajun's mind off her. "Where's your boss? It's Rabican I'm after."

"Back up against the wall," Dayka commanded. "Put your hands on your head."

Conscious of the red rivulet trickling down the woman's neck, Bolan obeyed. He placed his right hand on top of his left, doing it so casually, so skillfully, the Cajun never noticed his fingers slide up his left sleeve.

"That be better," Dayka said. "Now you stay there." Leaning forward, he slashed the rope that bound Nina's wrists. He wasn't gentle about it and nicked her left arm. Then, twisting to either side but never taking his eyes off Bolan, he did the same with the loops around her ankles. Instantly he pressed the blade to her throat again and made her stand in front of him. He wasn't taking any chances.

Nina's eyes were wide but not in fright. "You came after me, mister," she marveled. "You came all this way to help me?"

"Shut up!" Dayka barked. Dragging Nina with him, he sidestepped Mazoo's fallen form. A quick lunge, and he had the Browning in his left hand. "I should shoot you," he growled. His knife rose from Nina's throat and he shoved her to the floor. "I should shoot both of you."

Bolan gauged the distance and firmed his grip on the throwing knife under his sleeve.

"But the boss man, he'll want to see you, I be thinking," Dayka declared. "He'll want to question you." The Cajun glanced toward a desk in the corner. On it rested a cell phone.

Bolan began to ease the throwing knife from its sheath, ever so slowly, his entire body primed. Throwing a knife accurately required considerable skill, an ability he had honed over countless hours of practice. He was good enough to consistently hit the bull's-eye nine out of ten times. But there was no margin for error here.

Dayka pointed the Browning at Nina and warily backed toward the desk. "Try anything and the girl dies."

The Executioner had to give Dayka credit for being cagey. He had the throwing knife a third of the way out, but now Nina was between him and the Cajun.

Reaching the desk, Dayka dropped his knife onto it and groped for the cell phone without taking his eyes, or the Browning, off the woman. Finding it, he ran his forefinger over the buttons, getting the feel of which was which, and then started pressing them. He tapped the call key and raised the phone to his ear. All without looking at it. Someone at the other end had to have answered because Dayka rattled off a string of Cajun.

Bolan couldn't make much sense of what was being said. A lot was in the hybrid French-English mix peculiar to Dayka's kind. He gathered that the man had informed someone of his intervention and was requesting instructions. Dayka listened a bit, then said, "Is that true?" The whole time, the Browning's muzzle never dipped, and Dayka's finger rested on the inner edge of the trigger guard.

The Cajun finished talking. He set the phone on the desk and grinned. "They be sending people right quick. Belle wants to know who hired you and your friends to kill Rabican."

Bolan realized they had to think he was part of the hit squad that made the assault on the salt dome. Denying it would be pointless. "What does Belle have to do with this?" he played for time. "She's Rabican's girlfriend, I heard."

Dayka chortled. "That shows how much you know. Belle is much more. She is smart, that one. Smarter than Carbou. He hired you, didn't he? And you get this stupid girl to help you?"

"Nina isn't involved in any way."

"Sure she's not."

Neither of them anticipated what happened next. The Cajun still had the pistol trained on Nina, but he was looking at Bolan. She caught Dayka flatfooted when she catapulted herself up off the floor, screeching like an alley cat, and clawed at his face and eyes with her long painted fingernails.

Howling as much from pain as fury, Dayka tried to spring back, out of her reach, but he collided with the desk. Down he went, onto his back, with Nina on top of him. The Browning discharged, banging into the floor, not into her.

Bolan rushed to help. He couldn't throw the knife with her in the way. Darting to the right, he scooped up the Beretta and centered a quick bead on the Cajun's head, above the ear. But before he could shoot, Dayka rolled to the left and Nina slipped into his line of fire. He relaxed his trigger finger in the proverbial nick of time.

Nina had both hands on Dayka's right wrist and was holding on with a strength born of desperation, preventing him from using the pistol. In a burst of rage he slugged her with his other hand, but she clung on.

Bolan moved from one side to the other, seeking an unobstructed shot. For a moment he had one, but they rolled again, and Nina's shoulder rose into his sights. All too aware that the two sentries and whoever else was on the property were bound to have heard the shot and would investigate, he tried an unorthodox gambit. He took a long stride and leaped up over them, onto the top of the desk. Whirling, he stared down into Dayka's scowling features. The Cajun looked up, roared like a bear and made a superhuman effort to throw Nina off. He almost succeeded.

Extending the Beretta, Bolan placed a slug squarely in

the center of Dayka's forehead. Nina didn't realize the
Cajun was dead. Shrieking like a crazed she-wolf, she
ripped and tore at the man's eyes and cheeks and neck.

Jumping down, Bolan replaced the throwing knife, then
wrapped his left arm around both of hers, pinning her
gore-smeared hands to her sides. "He's dead!" he said in
her ear. "We've got to get out of here." Reinforcements
from Baton Rouge, if that was where Dayka had phoned,
would take a while to get there. Still, they couldn't waste
a minute.

Nina slumped, her adrenaline fading, her energy sapped.
"He was going to murder me," she said in quiet horror.
"And I thought he was my friend!"

Bolan snagged the cell phone and slid it into a pocket.
He took a moment to pick up the M-16, then, grabbing her
by the wrist, he pulled her erect and hurtled out the door
and down the hallway. From west of the building came
shouts. He hit the outer door with his shoulder and it exploded like a grenade.

A portly gunner Bolan hadn't seen before was only a
few yards off. The man stopped cold and raised the big
Ruger Redhawk in his pudgy right hand.

Bolan's Beretta fired once. Pulling Nina after him, he
bore to the left, keeping the corrugated building to his
back. Suddenly an Uzi sounded from the rear, the rounds
hitting the tin as loudly as hammers. He ducked, jerking
Nina down with him, as holes stitched a patchwork pattern
in the metal above their heads.

Throwing himself forward, Bolan let off two shots in the
direction of the sentries to discourage them. The Uzi
opened up again, but they were scrambling around the corner and the slugs missed.

Nina pressed herself to his side. She was quaking from

head to toe, her nails digging into his biceps. "I can't take this! Make them stop!"

"You did all right against Dayka," Bolan reminded her, hoping she wouldn't fall apart even more. Some people were so shaken by violence, they literally peed their pants or curled up into quivering mounds of mush and were easily slain. "Be strong and we'll make it."

"I'll try."

Forty feet directly ahead was the parking area. The locked gate was to their right. To the left, twenty-five yards or so, was another corrugated building, the largest of the three. "Hold this for me," Bolan said, shoving the Beretta into Nina's hands in the hope it might lend her some courage.

The Executioner unslung his M-16. They were now at the front of the middle building. The sentries were at the back. As soon as he stepped into the open, they would drop him. Well, he reflected wryly, that was why hand grenades were invented.

Plucking one from his pocket, Bolan spoke directly into the woman's right ear. "Hug the dirt and cover your ears. When I tug on your arm, run like hell for the last building. Understand?"

Nina was gaping at the grenade as if it were an A-bomb. "I swear to God," she said breathlessly, "if I make it out of here alive, I'm going to find a way to go to college and be a nurse like my mom wanted." She managed a feeble grin.

Bolan smiled in encouragement, then set down the rifle. The building was approximately 110 feet in length. A typical raw recruit could throw an M-67 fragmentation grenade about 120 feet. Under ideal conditions, he could hurl one about 160. So distance wasn't a problem. The trick was to have the grenade hit exactly where he wanted, in this case within a few feet of the rear wall. Between fragments from the grenade and shrapnel from the building, he should catch the two sentries in a blast no human being could possibly survive.

Bolan yanked out the pin. He had four to five seconds between the time he threw the grenade and when it would go off. Since he didn't want one of the sentries to try to hurl it back, he tossed it in a high overhand arc. It came down exactly where he wanted, a few feet behind the structure.

The explosion buffeted the air. Bolan had flung himself flat with one arm over his head and the other over Nina's. She mewed like a kitten, and her free hand gripped his thigh like a vise.

A screech rang out and from the mangled heap of corrugated tin flopped a single-limbed monstrosity. Both legs and one arm were gone, and the torso was leaking vital fluids like a punctured oil pan. The sentry flailed his lone arm and cried hysterically. Within seconds his cries dwindled and he died.

Had the blast nailed both sentries? That was the million-dollar question. Bolan pushed upright, the M-16 in his right hand, and sped toward the last building. Nina squawked as he yanked her off the ground. They covered ten yards without incident. Fifteen yards.

An Uzi ratcheted to life, spraying the space they had just occupied. Bolan spun in midstride, thinking it was the second sentry, but it was a new gunner, over by the parked vehicles. The driver of the limo, he reckoned, and he answered the Uzi with his rifle. He came close but not close enough, and the man ducked for cover behind the limo.

Only eight yards to go. Bolan weaved wildly to make it difficult for the gunners to get a lock. Nina did her best to imitate him, but she was frightened and couldn't match his on-a-dime turns in her high heels. To gain her precious moments, Bolan pushed her toward the third building even as he pivoted and raked the limousine and the second building with precisely controlled bursts.

Nina suddenly screamed.

A glance showed Bolan why. The door had opened and framed in it was a bruiser built like a Sherman tank. He was holding a double-barreled shotgun.

5

Strange sensations flooded through Tim Considine. He was both elated and surprised to find he was still alive. His head throbbed terribly, and it was an effort for him to think. A cool sensation on his skin perplexed him until he realized he was naked. He was laying on his back on a tiled surface, and his wrists were tied in front of him with soft cloth. Someone was busy binding his ankles. Nearby, water was running.

Considine opened his eyes and tried to sit up, but a blow to the chest slammed him back down.

"Don't even think it," Rico Fuentes said. He had cut one of Considine's towels into strips using a switchblade that lay on the floor near Considine's feet. "Don't yell, either, or I'll make it worse on you."

"What do you think you're doing?" Considine demanded. They were in his bathroom, and the running water he had heard was his bathtub being filled.

"You know, for a brainiac, you're not too smart." Fuentes completed a knot and retrieved the switchblade. "Are you going to tell me you haven't figured it out?" Fuentes closed the switchblade and shoved it into a pants pocket. "Aren't you embarrassed to die so dumb?"

Considine stared at the water pouring from the spout, at the cloth strips that wouldn't leave bruises no matter how hard he strained and stark fear coalesced deep inside him. "You wouldn't dare," he croaked.

"Why? Because you're a big shot who has the ear of the President?" Fuentes laughed. "Man, you are too lame to be believed. What do I care? They'll never be able to pin this on me. A year from now, when I have a million dollars in the bank and I'm sipping rum on the sands of Barbados, I'll hoist a drink in your memory."

The renegade Marine's comments were like icy barbs that pierced Considine to his marrow. "You're wrong if you think my superiors won't figure it out. They know all about you, all about every one of you. There's no place you can hide."

Fuentes rose and sat on the edge of the tub. "Nice try. But Maddy says you've been putting us on. That the only one who knows about the Scorpions is you."

A terrible weakness radiated from Considine's abdomen. "What makes her think a thing like that?"

"She did some snooping around. There's no record of us at the NIC. No record of us anywhere that she could find except in your personal records." Fuentes grinned like a Cheshire cat. "She had me break in here and make copies of those disks you have hidden away in that big book."

The weakness was worse, and Considine's mouth was terribly dry. "How on earth did you find them?"

"We were trained to be the best, weren't we? All of those

classes you had us attend on espionage and counterespionage techniques. So you could say I found the disks
thanks to you." Fuentes dipped a finger into the tub. "Another couple of inches and it will be high enough for your
'accident.'"

Panic welled, and Considine nearly opened his mouth
to shout for help. But it wouldn't do to show weakness. He
still had the upper hand. They just didn't know it. Rolling
onto his side with his back to Fuentes, he hiked his knees
to his stomach to cover his groin.

"What, are you the shy type?"

"Listen to me, Rico. It's not too late. Cut me loose, help
me deal with Maddy, and we'll pretend this never happened. It will be business as usual."

"What business?" Fuentes responded. "The business
where we go out and put our butts on the line for God,
country and peanuts? Or the business where we whack
badasses for four hundred thou a pop? My cut is one hundred thousand per job. How much do you make a year?"

"There's more to life than money," Considine said.

Fuentes had the whitest teeth. "What planet are you
from? Money is *all* that matters. Maddy has figured out
how each of us can be filthy rich, and I, for one, can't fill
my pockets soon enough."

"I gave you a second chance. I brought you into the fold
so you could redeem yourself in the eyes of your country-
men and your President—"

"Don't start with that crap again," Fuentes said irrita-
bly. "It's bogus. We're on to your act. The real reason you
picked four losers like us is because we're expendable. No
one will raise a stink if we buy the farm."

"That's not true."

"Maddy has your whole scam figured out. And we don't

want any part of it. That's why we've gone freelance. That's why you're about to see how long you can hold your breath."

Considine racked his brain for a convincing argument. "The four of you have done a lot of good. You've stopped tons of drugs from reaching kids on the street. You've checked the spread of illegal arms throughout Europe. You've—"

Fuentes dismissed their accomplishments with an impatient flick of his wrist. "I don't give a damn about any of that." He thumped his chest. "All I care about is me."

"But you were a Marine."

"So? You make it sound like I was a saint or something," Fuentes scoffed, then turned off the water. "The only reason I went into the Marines was to beat a robbery rap. The police were breathing down my neck. I figured they'd let it slide once they heard I was in the service."

Considine saw Fuentes reach for one last strip, the strip that would be applied as a gag. It was time to drop the boom. "Hear me out. Do you honestly believe I'm stupid enough not to have a contingency plan for a scenario exactly like this? Do you think it never occurred to me some of you might go bad? I've taken certain steps, and unless you let me go, you'll find yourself hunted down and killed."

"Do you know what I think, big brain?" Fuentes asked. "I think you're lying. Trying to scare me into sparing your sorry life. But it won't work."

"You're making the biggest mistake of your life," Considine warned. There must be a way of convincing Fuentes he was sincere, Considine thought. He refused to accept he was about to die. Not after all his careful planning. "What if I give you a phone number to call? Ask the man who answers whether I'm telling the truth or not."

"How stupid do you think I am?" Fuentes slid off the tub onto his knees. "Time to get this over with, boss man. Go ahead and yell if it will make you feel any better."

Considine fell for the ruse. He threw back his head to shout for help, and just like that, Fuentes shoved the wadded strip of cloth into his mouth, effectively stifling his outcry. He tried to spit it out, but it was wedged fast. Gagging, he coughed and sputtered. Fuentes's arm slid under his knees and another around his back, and the NIC man lashed out with both legs, seeking to knock the smaller man aside.

"I don't mind you fighting. I'd do the same." Fuentes lifted him with unbelievable ease and held him over the tub. "You know the routine. We want this to look like an accident, like you slipped and hit your head on the side of the tub and drowned. That whack I gave you on the head has bruised nicely. Now for the finishing touch."

Fright so potent it chilled Considine's blood spiked through him. Frantically he bucked and heaved, but the smaller man merely smiled.

"Struggle all you want. There won't be any marks on your wrists or ankles. You're about to become a statistic, one of the hundreds who die in bathtub accidents every year." Fuentes began to lower him. "Not exactly the kind of death you imagined, I bet. But we never get to pick how and when."

Considine didn't care to hear it. He didn't care about stupid statistics. All he cared about was living. He tried to butt Fuentes with his head, but the former Marine jerked back. He sought to knee Fuentes in the face but couldn't move his legs far enough. In a final act of sheer panic, Considine wrenched his entire body to one side to break free, and succeeded all too well. With a loud splash he fell into the tub.

The water closed above him, seeping into his nostrils. He levered upward and for a few seconds his nose was above the surface and he could breathe. Then a callused hand was pressed against his chest.

"Too bad you're not a fish," Fuentes said.

Tim Considine whimpered as he was shoved back under. Again wetness filled his nostrils. He held his breath, gaining himself an extra minute or two. Placing his feet flat on the bottom of the tub, he heaved upward. But Fuentes had both hands on his chest, and he couldn't rise more than a couple of inches. Again and again he tried, pumping upward in a frenzy. He twisted. He tried to kick both legs out over the rim for extra purchase. Nothing worked. His lungs felt fit to burst, and although he didn't want to, although he resisted with every iota of willpower, his body wouldn't be denied. He breathed water.

Considine saw Rico Fuentes's distorted face above him. He wished it was Maddy Culver. He wished he could get his hands around her scrawny neck and throttle her until she was dead. He wished he had never picked her. Wished he had never come up with the idea for the Scorpions. His vision blurred, and his body seemed to fold in on itself. All sensation faded. His last wish was that his contingency plan worked and he saw them all in hell.

THE EXECUTIONER and the man in the doorway of the third building both leveled their weapons at the same moment. But Bolan was a hair faster. The M-16 spit lead in a tight arc, the slugs creating a half-moon pattern in the bruiser's flannel shirt. The man staggered back, his Mossberg pistol-grip shotgun discharging into the ground and blowing a hole as big as a cantaloupe. The recoil toppled him onto his back, blood spouting from half a dozen wounds.

Nina froze in consternation and glanced at Bolan, unsure whether to go on. A shove sent her toward the front of the building. The guy over by the vehicles and the second sentry both reentered the fray, their Uzis chattering ferociously, but they were firing from the hip ferociously. They weren't trained soldiers, and neither scored a hit.

Bolan and Nina darted around the corner and dropped onto their knees, Nina wheezing as if she had asthma. "We'll never get out of this! There are too many!"

"We don't know how many there are," Bolan said. He glanced at a window above them but it was dark, the blinds down. "Try not to panic."

"You must be joking." Nina was wide-eyed and pale, her fear threatening to eclipse her reason. "I've never been shot at before. The panic comes naturally."

"I'll get you out of this if you can stay calm."

"You don't ask much, do you?"

Bolan motioned for her to be quiet. He was trying to work out what to do. There were three ways out of the place. Through the gate, which was padlocked. Through the hole the dog had made, which was at the far side of the compound. Or over the fence. But the barbed wire at the top of the fence would hinder them too much, and make them sitting ducks.

A fourth alternative was to eliminate the rest of the shooters. If he was alone, Bolan wouldn't mind going up against as many men as they threw at him. But he had the woman to think of. She was an innocent caught up in his private war, and he would be damned if he would let any harm come to her. Protecting her was his paramount priority.

Bolan inched to the edge of the corner. The driver had gone to ground among the vehicles. A grenade would take care of him, but Bolan had a better idea. The keys to the limo were either inside it or the driver had them.

The limo was their ticket out of there.

Nina had her arms wrapped around her knees, and she was trembling like an aspen leaf in a gale. Placing a hand on her shoulder, Bolan whispered, "When I give the word, we're going to make a break for the limousine. Stay close behind me and keep low."

"You have a plan?" she hopefully inquired.

"I always have a plan." Bolan wasn't bragging. Tactics were second nature to him. Years of unending combat in killing fields all over the globe had ingrained an aptitude for devising instant strategies to counter any situation. Hal Brognola once commented, only half in jest, that Bolan's mind was like one of those computer games programmed to play chess. Only in his case, Bolan had learned every combat tactic and trick there was, and then some.

Swiveling on the balls of his feet, Bolan took out the spotlight nearest the parking area with a single shot. He gave the one closest to them the same treatment. A third light merited the same treatment. Now the front third of the fenced area was mantled in darkness.

Belatedly Rabican's triggermen realized Bolan was up to something and decided to dissuade him. The driver popped up, his Uzi hammering. The second sentry fired from somewhere to the rear of the second building. And a third gunner, previously unsuspected, began banging away with a large-caliber rifle from over by the far fence.

Bolan ducked back as rounds peppered the tin. He couldn't say what made him glance at the window again. Maybe it was a hint of movement. Maybe it was his intuition blaring. Maybe it was dumb luck. Whatever the case, he spotted another hardcase who had parted the blinds and was taking deliberate aim at his back with a big revolver.

Spinning, Bolan threw himself onto his side. The revolver boomed, and the window showered outward in a spray of tiny shards of glass.

Nina screamed.

The Executioner elevated the M-16, flicking the selector lever from semiauto to full-auto as he did. He squeezed the trigger and held it down.

An M-16 on automatic was capable of firing from 150 to 200 rounds per minute; Bolan's magazine held thirty rounds. In a span of less than ten seconds he emptied it into the back shooter.

The man jerked and twitched as if he were being subjected to an electric shock. His face and upper chest dissolved into a pockmarked travesty of a human being. Dead on his feet, he collapsed the instant the M-16 went dry. His arms and neck became entangled in the blinds and he hung there, swaying from side to side, blood oozing like dark pus.

Without missing a beat, Bolan ejected the spent magazine and slapped home a new one. The firing from other quarters had stopped. He carefully took a peek. The other three gunners were lying low, biding their time, waiting for him to make the next move. A move he had to make soon.

Bolan had figured the reinforcements being sent would take a good hour to get there, but it wasn't etched in concrete. Maybe they were nearer than Baton Rouge. In which case they might arrive at any moment.

The parking area was mired in shadow. Bolan darkened the area even more by taking out two more lights along the perimeter fence. He was almost ready. He palmed his second grenade.

"Not one of those again," Nina said.

"We need a distraction, and I'm fresh out of firecrackers." Bolan's attempt at humor failed to produce a grin. Pulling the pin, he tensed for the throw. He couldn't reach the gunner at the rear of the second building or the rifleman by the fence, but he didn't need to. All he had to do was divert their attention from the parking area. To that end, he rose, cocked his arm and threw the grenade with all his might. It sailed high and true, striking the roof of the second building with a thump.

The blast rivaled the first. Tin ruptured skyward with a great rending screech, and the entire center section of the structure convulsed.

Bolan was in motion before the din died. He checked to confirm Nina was right behind him. Bent low, they raced toward the vehicles. The gunners had to have fallen for his ploy and were staring at the second building; not a single shot rang out. He reached the sedan at the near end of the parking lot and pulled Nina down beside him.

Flames had spouted from the middle building and were licking at the buckled walls. The triggerman at the rear shouted something, but Bolan couldn't quite catch the words.

The soldier stalked around the sedan to the Jeep. Nina was practically breathing down his neck. He dropped onto his hands and knees and peered underneath. A pair of shoes were visible under the limo, near the front tire on the driver's side.

Uncurling, Bolan placed a finger to his lips and gestured for Nina to stay where she was. He glided around the Jeep to the trunk of the limo. It gave him a clear shot at the driver, who was mesmerized by the conflagration engulfing the building.

The man never heard the soldier sneak up on him, never

had any inkling Bolan was there until the M-16 was jammed into the base of his spine.

"Pretend you're a statue," Bolan growled.

The driver had stiffened and foolishly started to turn but caught himself. "Don't kill me!" he bleated.

"You were all set to kill us," Bolan said. Jabbing the rifle harder, he reached past the driver's hip and relieved him of the Uzi. "Tell me where the limo's keys are."

"In my pants."

"Hand them over." Bolan slid the Uzi under the limo. "Nice and slow."

"I was only doing what I'm paid to do," the driver said as he gingerly inserted several fingers into a pocket. "Nothing personal, right?"

"Save the whitewash and shut up," Bolan snapped. Following orders was always the excuse of last resort. The Nazis had used it to justify the holocaust, the Romans to justify slaughtering Christians. Fascists and Communists adopted it as their mantra. And while it was true that good soldiers always did as they were told, there was more to soldiering than following orders. Soldiers had to have a sense of right and wrong. They had to remember a higher authority took precedence over an order to perform an evil act. Some called it conscience. Some called it the soul. Others said it was the will of God. To Bolan, it was all three wrapped into one.

The driver produced a key ring and Bolan snatched it from his grasp. "Please don't kill me!" he repeated.

"Turn around."

The driver did as he was directed. He wasn't more than eighteen or nineteen, a boy seduced by the lure of drugs, guns and the fast life into the role of hired muscle, for which he was patently ill-suited.

"When I tell you, I want you to run toward the north fence and shout your head off," Bolan instructed him.

"What do you want me to yell?" the boy nervously asked.

"Anything. Just so your friends can see and hear you."

The driver's eyes darted toward where his friends were hidden. "But they might gun me down by mistake!"

"That's your problem," Bolan said, nudging him. "Get going. Don't look back and don't stop."

"Oh God!" The young man gulped, thrust both arms above his head and bolted around the front of the limo, bawling, "Don't shoot! Don't shoot! Don't shoot! Don't shoot!"

Bolan grabbed the doorknob and yanked. Throwing himself across the front seat, he flung the passenger door open and hollered, "Nina! Get in! Keep low!" With any luck, the gunners were watching the antics of their friend and wouldn't notice. He glanced toward the rear of the Jeep, expecting her to come around it. But she had a different idea. She came *through* it, first opening the opposite door, then sliding over the bucket seats and barreling out the near door almost into his arms.

Slipping behind the steering wheel, Bolan laid the M-16 between them. Four keys were on the key ring. The second started the engine. Throwing the shift lever into Drive, Bolan tramped on the gas pedal. The tires squealed as he slewed the limousine in a semicircle. Shouts greeted the maneuver. So did gunfire. The side window was hit. The trunk was hammered by autofire.

Bolan aimed the grille at the locked gate and kept the pedal floored. "Get down!" he cried.

Nina flattened against the seat.

The stretch limo was a turtle compared to most cars. Its size, its bulk, lent it the racing characteristics of a brick. But it was the next best thing to having a tank. The speedometer climbed to twenty miles per hour, then to twenty-five. "Faster!" Bolan whispered, and the needle jumped to forty.

Like a living battering ram, the limousine smashed into the gate. The chain shattered under the massive impact and the two halves of the gate flew outward, the right half ripped from its hinges. Bolan spun the wheel and veered onto the dirt road, the rear end swerving wildly.

It wouldn't take the remaining gunners long to jump into the other vehicles and give chase. Bolan pushed the limo to fifty, to sixty, to sixty-five. When his rental materialized in his headlights, he slammed on the brakes.

"Why are you stopping?" Nina asked. She was peering over the seat toward the phony landscape company.

"The other car is faster." Bolan swerved the limousine sideways across the road, effectively blocking it, and leaped out. Nina slid out his side rather than her own, and nearly blundered into him when he abruptly stopped. Taking her by the shoulders, he pushed her past him and turned toward the limo.

"What are you doing?"

Bolan let the M-16 speak for him. Leveling it, he shot out the tires on their near side, then, as an added measure, drilled the hood with a dozen rounds.

Nina smiled. "I get it! You blocked the road so they can't chase us. That's pretty smart."

The soldier didn't have the heart to tell her it wouldn't delay the smugglers all that long.

At least, not if they used the Jeep. Thanks to its four-wheel-drive capability, it could swing wide, into the swamp, and wouldn't get bogged down. He hustled her to his rental and opened the passenger door. "Let's go."

Two headlights flared to life north of them. Taking the Jeep, the gunners whisked through the shattered gate and raced in pursuit.

Bolan slid into the Taurus, shoved the M-16 at Nina and gunned the engine. Executing a U-turn, he raced off. He had plenty of gas, and the Taurus had enough horsepower to hold its own, so he couldn't foresee being caught unless fickle fate intervened. "You can relax a little," he said.

"Just a little?" Nina said critically. "I was hoping you'd say we're completely out of danger."

"Not yet." Bolan was thinking of the reinforcements, the unknown factor that could spoil everything. He peaked the speedometer at seventy-five and held it there. Plumes of dust and gravel cascaded in their wake.

Nina's fingers found his arm. "I want to thank you for what you've done. No one has ever gone to so much trouble for me before."

"It was my fault they took you," Bolan said.

"How do you figure? I was the one who picked you up outside the bar, remember? The only one to blame is me. And the lesson I've learned will keep me off the streets for the rest of my life."

Bolan hoped she was serious. "That nurse idea sounded good. Not many nurses are dragged from hospitals and tortured."

Nina gave rein to peals of mirth far in excess of what the quip deserved. One hand on the dash, she laughed and laughed.

The soldier chalked it up to frayed nerves. When she stopped, she did so abruptly, almost as if the laughter had caught in her throat.

"What's that light in the sky?"

To the northeast an artificial star was bearing in their general direction. A small plane, Bolan guessed, and mentally crossed his fingers it was a routine civilian flight. The aircraft altered its course slightly, and he could see other lights. The configuration identified it as helicopter, not a plane. At twice their speed it swept in low over the swamp to their rear, banked directly over the sedan and the Jeep, then steadied and streaked toward them.

"It's after us!" Nina yelled.

6

To some people Hal Brognola appeared to have the perfect job. He was part of the inner circle of shakers and movers in U.S. government. His influence behind the scenes, his prestige among his peers, were second to none. He traveled a lot. He received a more than adequate income. And with his job came a wealth of other fabulous perks, from chauffeured limos—if so desired—to a private jet reserved exclusively for his use.

To casual outsiders Brognola might seem to have all anyone could want. But they weren't aware of the eighteen-hour days he routinely put in. They had no idea of the grave crises he faced, day in and day out. They didn't realize the monumental weight on his shoulders—the welfare of every man, woman and child in the United States of America.

Not that Brognola ever complained. The responsibility

came with the territory. He was proud to serve his country in whatever capacity he was able. And he was never happier than when he thwarted another assault on the country he cherished and the ideals for which she stood.

After talking to Bolan, Brognola had buzzed Agent Farrow and asked her to do a computer rundown on any and all intel relating to four-person military-type hit squads reported over the past six months. What she found stunned him. Six months ago in Paris, the head of Perigord Industries had been murdered by four people who displayed what a newspaper reporter characterized as "military-style precision." Security cameras had caught the culprits on film, but they were never identified. Five months ago, in Turkey, a major narcotics trafficker had been gunned down on the streets of Izmir by four assailants in combat fatigues who vanished into thin air within walking distance of the U.S. Embassy. Three months ago a right-wing military thug in Peru had been silenced by a four-person hit squad believed to be composed of renegade Peruvian officers. Two months past, in Ireland, an IRA hothead who stood in the way of peace initiatives was treated to a special lead diet by four people who jumped out of a truck, gunned him down and were gone before bystanders had recovered their wits.

Brognola spread the reports out across his desk and read through them again. "It can't be," he said aloud. Yet there was no denying the pattern. All were prominent targets with interests inimical to the U.S. All had been disposed of by a four-man hit squad. Four-*person* was more accurate, since it was established beyond a shadow of a doubt one of the four was a woman. He stabbed his intercom. "Agent Farrow?"

"Sir?"

"Broaden your search and go back a full year." Brognola reflected a moment. "Make that two years. Have Agent Jennings assist you. And I want it on my desk an hour ago."

"Yes, sir."

Lacing his fingers behind his head, Brognola pondered the implications of what they had uncovered so far. Based on the evidence, the U.S. now had its own version of those South American death squads that occasionally made the headlines. The overriding question for him was whether the death squad was sanctioned. If so, it opened a horrendous can of worms. If not, then whoever was responsible had to be put out of business as soon as practical.

Despite himself, Brognola had to admire their efficiency. Four hits in six months, carried out flawlessly. And who knew how many more?

Brognola prayed it wasn't a sanctioned op. It would mean someone was encroaching on his territory, on the exclusive purview of the ultracovert Stony Man Farm and its dedicated personnel. Stony Man was supposed to be a one-of-a-kind operation answerable only to him and the President.

A sudden thought jarred Brognola into sitting up straight. His outlook smacked of hypocrisy. The death squad was doing the same thing Bolan did. So why was it okay for him and not for them? Some might argue that in permitting a man like Mack Bolan to have carte blanche, the U.S. government was effectively endorsing vigilantism.

Brognola begged to differ. Bolan was unique. A living weapon unleashed only when all other avenues had been exhausted or when the threat was so great or so immediate that working through normal channels would be the equivalent of too little, too late.

Brognola made no apologies for his friend's activities. They fell under the umbrella of moral necessity.

THE HELICOPTER HAD BEEN painted black and bore no markings, a legal violation in itself. Bolan got a look at it in the rearview mirror as it streaked low along the dirt road toward them.

He identified the whirlybird as a McDonnell Douglas Model 300. Good news, in that it was a commercial model and not a warbird. But a gunner was leaning out of the cockpit, and he was cradling what appeared to be a Browning Automatic Rifle.

The next second the road beside Bolan erupted in a chain of earthen geysers. Over the whine of the Taurus's engine he heard the metallic rattle of the BAR. Instantly he swerved to the left. More geysers sprouted where the car had just been, then danced toward it. But an extra burst of gas spared them from harm, and the chopper whipped by and climbed for another strafing run.

As if the helicopter weren't enough to contend with, the Jeep had fishtailed around the limousine and was still giving chase.

"You need to take the wheel," Bolan told Nina.

"Me?" She gawked as if he were insane. "I'm not that great a driver. Hell, I don't even own a car."

"I can't shoot and drive at the same time."

"I'm sorry. I'd only get us killed that much sooner." Nina backed against her door. "Please. Don't make me do it. You'll have to get us out of this yourself."

Bolan frowned and bent forward over the steering wheel. The helicopter was looping wide to come at them head-on. There would be no avoiding it, no evading the rain of death. Not unless he braked and they made a dash for the swamp. But then the men in the Jeep would be after them. And with Nina to slow him, their prospects for survival were slim.

Coming to a decision, Bolan stomped on the brake pedal. The car skidded to a halt, raising a cloud of dust that would screen them from view of the Jeep.

"What are you doing?" Nina had flung both hands against the dash to keep from being thrown through the windshield. "Why are we stopping?"

Bolan switched off the headlights and shut off the engine. Grabbing the M-16, he jumped out. From the air their car was now next to invisible. In order to locate them, the pilot had to reduce airspeed. As Bolan intended. Running quickly to the trunk, Bolan grabbed the combo M-16/M-203. After loading one round into the breech, the Executioner waited.

The helicopter dipped low over the road. The pilot and the gunner were trying to pinpoint the Taurus in all the dust and the gloom. They weren't more than fifty feet in the air, perilously low considering the number of trees that flanked the roadway.

Bolan glued his eyes to the cockpit. He had an M-406 high explosive round in the breech. It had an effective blast radius of fifteen feet or more. But it was made to detonate on impact. He had to hit the chopper dead-on, or the grenade would sail past and go off when it struck the ground.

Another complication was the time delay. An M-406 didn't arm itself until it had traveled roughly forty-five feet.

Bolan had to take all that into account, as well as trajectory and elevation. Luckily windage wasn't a factor this night. He flipped up the launcher's sight leaf, which was fitted to the top of the handguard. Ingeniously designed, the sight leaf had what was known as an open ladder series of sights that allowed for rapid firing without having to repeatedly adjust it.

The range indicator numbers on either side of the leaf were barely visible. Bolan tracked the helicopter, leading it by a good margin, wanting it closer before he let fly. He wished it would drop a little lower, and the next second the pilot dipped the aircraft another fifteen feet. It was a mistake someone with combat experience would never make.

Bolan now had a new option. Instead of trying to hit the chopper in midair, which was akin to trying to hit a clay pigeon with a BB, he could fire at the ground in front of it. Even if the blast didn't knock the whirlybird out of the sky, the grenade was bound to cause extensive damage.

Lowering the M-16/M-203 combo, Bolan sighted on a spot about forty yards ahead of the onrushing craft.

The gunner spotted him. The Browning rifle barked, rounds kicking up dust in a beeline for where he stood. The Executioner took a step to the right and the lead danced past, narrowly missing him, the car and Nina.

"My turn," Bolan said, then stroked the launcher's trigger.

The grenade hit where he wanted it to. Caught with his pants down, the pilot flew right into the blast. The chopper was enveloped in a spewing cloud of concussive force. It swerved violently westward, out over the swamp, the rotor canting wildly. Ragged holes speckled the cockpit. The gunner was clinging to the door frame for dear life while the pilot fought the stick to bring the chopper under control.

Bolan didn't linger. The Jeep was still bearing down on them. Diving behind the steering wheel, he started the car and went from zero to sixty in what had to be a record for a Taurus.

The chopper hovered 150 yards out, or was trying to. The fuselage swayed from side to side like a pendulum gone amok, and the engine was keening and making clanging sounds.

"You did it!" Nina said in pure awe, her face pressed to her window. "I'm beginning to think you can do anything."

If she only knew, Bolan thought, glancing into the rearview mirror. The Jeep had gained a lot of ground and was now sixty or seventy yards behind them. He pushed the speedometer to seventy-five, to eighty.

Nina looked at him in wonder. "Where did you learn to do all this stuff?"

"I don't have time to answer a lot of questions," Bolan responded. Popping sounds from the rear alerted him someone in the Jeep was anxious to stop them. As for the chopper, it had fallen well behind and was limping toward solid ground.

Nina paid him no heed. "Where did you learn to kill people like you do? How is it you have all this military stuff?" She leaned toward him. "And has anyone ever mentioned you have the most adorable blue eyes?"

Bolan glanced at her. He couldn't decide if she was serious or not, but it didn't matter. "I need to concentrate. Sit there and keep quiet."

"My, my," Nina said, miffed. "Aren't you the grumpy Gus? You're the one who told me I could relax a little, and now that I am, you're jumping down my throat."

"We're not out of the woods yet," Bolan stressed.

"So? After what you did to that helicopter, I have every confidence in you." Nina reached out and touched his hand. "When this is over, maybe you and I can finish having that drink together. I'll treat you to a time you'll never forget."

There they were, racing pell-mell through the dark of a Louisiana swamp, being shot at by smugglers, and she had romance on her mind? Bolan shook his head in exasperation. Men liked to joke that women were from another planet, or vice versa, and at times like this he was inclined to agree. Then again, he had saved her life, and it was a documented psychological fact that victims of violent crime and natural calamities often developed a crush on the policemen, firemen and paramedics who saved them.

Without warning, the junction appeared out of the murk. Mad at himself for his lapse of attention, Bolan applied the brakes and furiously churned the steering wheel. The car went into a slide. Vegetation on the other side of the road loomed toward them, and Bolan heard Nina's sharp intake of breath. With inches to spare, the vehicle lurched to a stop. And the engine stalled.

Bolan turned the key. The starter made a grinding noise but the engine wouldn't kick over. He tried again, wary of flooding it.

The Jeep was barreling toward them like a demented bat out of Hades. Someone was leaning out the passenger side.

"Hurry!" Nina urged.

Again Bolan tried the ignition. This time the car sputtered and coughed, but it still wouldn't cooperate. His door thudded to the impact of multiple slugs, low down on the panel.

"They're shooting at us!"

The third time was the charm. The Taurus roared, and Bolan tried to shove his foot through the floor. He accelerated so fast, he was slapped against the seat. So was Nina, who laughed as if it were a carnival ride. Given a choice between having her relaxed or so scared she couldn't move, he'd rather it was the latter.

The Jeep took the turn on two wheels. The moment it straightened, the gunner peppered their trunk.

"He couldn't hit the broad side of a barn," Nina stated with a bliss born of total ignorance. "He keeps missing us."

"But he's getting our range," Bolan said.

"He is?"

That shut her up for a while. Bolan increased his lead by a dozen yards, enough to discourage their pursuers from wasting lead. He glanced to the northwest but couldn't spot the helicopter. It had to have landed. He wondered if its radio still worked, and if the pilot had gotten on the horn to Rabican. What if more reinforcements were on their way? It might be wise to consider an alternate route back to Baton Rouge.

"Mister! Look out!"

Nina's scream snapped Bolan's head around. He saw what he took for a log in the center of the road, then realized the log was moving. He hit the brakes but there wasn't enough stopping room. At forty-five miles per hour the car plowed into the alligator. The front end lifted and they went airborne. Nina screamed louder.

Bolan hadn't had time to put on his seat belt. Bracing himself against the steering wheel, he hoped for the best. They came down hard. His head slammed against the roof, and he was pitched toward Nina. Clinging to the steering wheel with one hand, he struggled to keep the car on an even keel. It was swerving from road edge to road edge, tires shrieking.

"A tree!" Nina wailed.

Avoiding it was impossible. The best Bolan could do was angle the Taurus so the point of impact was on his side of the car. Metal crumpled like paper. Momentum clubbed him against the dashboard and pain spiked his left arm from the elbow to the shoulder. The barrel of the M-16 scraped his temple. A foot was shoved into his face, and a high heel raked his cheek.

Then all was still. Bolan sat up and took stock. He was

battered but unhurt. Nina had been upended and was on her butt on the floor. Her hair was askew and she looked about to cry. "Are you all right?" he asked. Gripping her hand, he pulled her onto the seat.

"I think so." She was dazed, her speech slurred. "Give me a minute to catch my breath. My stomach is in my throat."

They didn't have a minute. The Jeep was swinging wide of the stricken gator and would be on them before they knew it. Bolan shoved his door open, clutched the rifle and her arm, and bustled out. They were on a reed-choked bank. Below lay a limpid pool.

Wrapping his arm around Nina's slim waist, Bolan leaped. They cleared the reeds and landed with a splash, creating a rippling wave. Slanting to the right, Bolan took six long strides, then ducked into the reeds. Squatting, he drew Nina down close to him.

Bright light swept over the bank and their wrecked vehicle. The throaty purr of the Jeep's engine drowned out the frogs and crickets, and brakes squeaked noisily. Shadowy forms moved toward the pool, and three gunners materialized on top of the bank.

"They went into the swamp!" one man blurted as if astounded anyone would be so foolhardy.

"Anton, you and Bogger go after them."

"Like hell. I ain't going in that water at night. Snakes are all over the place. And you saw that gator yonder. He might have kin close by."

"I wasn't asking you," the middle gunner said. "I was telling you."

"Who do you think you are? Belle?"

Bolan settled the argument for them with three short bursts. The hardmen jerked and tottered and died. He listened for footsteps, for whispers, but if there were any, the Jeep's engine smothered them. "Stay here," he whispered.

"Not on your life!" Nina responded. "I felt something crawl past my leg a second ago."

The reeds rustled slightly as Bolan moved up the bank, his M-16 sweeping from side to side. He climbed slowly, cautiously. There might be more gunners just waiting for him to poke his head above the bank. He listened, but heard only the hiss of steam escaping from the Taurus's crushed radiator.

A brown shoe jutted at the stars. Attached to it was a jean-clad leg, and to the leg a chest stained red by spreading blood. Nearby were the other bodies, sprawled like disjointed scarecrows.

"You got all of them!" Nina whooped.

Bolan gave her a look that implied he would rip her throat out if she didn't keep her mouth shut. Springing up over the bank, he moved to the Taurus, keeping it between him and the Jeep. Both of the Jeep's front doors were open. No one was inside. He probed the surrounding area and came up empty. "You can come out now," he called out when he was positive it was safe.

Nina stepped to the first body and studied the triggerman's swarthy features. "You know, I never saw a dead person before tonight. They look like they're sleeping, don't they?"

Bolan opened the Taurus's passenger door, reclaimed the keys and moved to the trunk. Nine holes sprinkled its surface. Opening the lid, he shouldered the strap to his duffel bag. He tossed it into the back of the Jeep and climbed in.

A cell phone was on the dash. He added it to his collection, shifted into Reverse and looked at Nina. "Are you coming, or do you want to camp out here overnight?"

"Not so far. Aren't you going to check these guys for identification and things like that?"

"Why bother? The authorities will see to it their next of

kin are notified." Bolan wasn't a policeman or a federal agent, and that was their province. Patting the bucket seat beside him, he said, "Get in before you step on a snake."

Nina looked down, then darted to the passenger door. "I swear," she said, sliding in, "I'm never leaving the city again as long as I live. People can have the country. All the creepy-crawlies give me the willies."

Bolan worked the gear lever and drove past the Taurus. Steam continued to rise from the shattered radiator, and a puddle of fluid was forming under the engine block. He brought the Jeep to the speed limit. "In less than an hour you'll be home, safe and sound."

"I don't know if I'll ever feel safe again," Nina said, running her slender fingers through her hair. "What's to stop Rabican and his bullies from coming after me again? They're not going to like what you've done, and they'll think it's partly my fault, I bet."

"I won't let them hurt you," Bolan assured her. "But I need you to lie low for a week or two. Is there somewhere you can go? Somewhere they would never think to look?"

"I have an aunt in Chicago who I haven't seen in years." Nina said. "I suppose I could pay her a surprise visit. But I don't have the price of a bus ticket."

"Maybe I can help," Bolan stated. He had close to two thousand in expense money. Fifty-dollar bills were better than credit cards. They didn't leave a paper trail for a computer to trace.

"You never answered my question," Nina said. "Why are you going to all this trouble on my account?"

"You needed help."

"That's all there is to it?" Nina was incredulous. "You're willing to risk your life for someone you hardly know? What kind of man are you?"

Bolan didn't answer.

Nina stared at him a while, thoughtfully gnawing on her lower lip. "The last of a dying breed," she said at length and smiled self-consciously. "I heard that somewhere once. It must have stuck in my head."

Bolan had seen the same movie. Henry Fonda had been one of his favorite actors back in the days when he had spare time to go to movies and watch television. He rarely did either nowadays. He rarely read books for enjoyment's sake. Rarely read magazines. They had been added to the long list of personal sacrifices he'd been forced to make.

Bolan became aware Nina was still talking to him.

"...anyone like you in my entire life. Too bad there aren't more where you come from. Speaking for women everywhere, I am sick to death of geeks and boys pretending to be men."

One of the cell phones in Bolan's pockets rang, interrupting her. It was the phone he had taken from the landscaping company. He pressed the Receive button and held the phone to his ear. "Yeah?"

"Dayka?" a woman's sultry voice purred in his ear. "About time you answered. What in hell is going on out there?" The caller didn't wait for an answer. "I sent Jacko in the helicopter and roused Keefer. He was close. He and his boys should be at Canbiar in about fifteen minutes."

Bolan glanced up. Off down the road a pair of headlights had appeared.

"Hold out until Keefer gets there," the voice said. "That crazy bastard will take care of the man who has been meddling in our affairs. I guarantee."

7

Hal Brognola considered the computer a godsend. Before the computer age, law enforcement was hampered by the plodding pace of paperwork. Routine background checks took weeks to perform. The ability to exchange detailed information with other departments was at the mercy of the U.S. mail. Contacting agencies overseas required even more patience. In short, the wheels of justice ground exceedingly slow, and law enforcement suffered as a result.

Along came the computer, and all that changed. Background checks were completed in minutes. Contacting other countries was as simple as obtaining the right E-mail address. Best of all, a treasure trove of intel was a few keystrokes away.

Agents Farrow and Jennings were computer wizards when it came to research. Forty-five minutes after Brognola set them to their task, Farrow knocked on his door and deposited an inch-thick manila folder on his desk. It contained news accounts as well as police and Army reports on dozens of slayings worldwide in which the common denominator was a mysterious hit squad. Sometimes only three people were seen, sometimes fewer, but it didn't take a great stretch of logic to imagine the others were always on the scene, providing backup, if nothing else.

Brognola spent more than an hour going over them one by one and arranging them in chronological order. A few facts became clear. The hits had started a year and a half earlier with a renegade arms dealer in Kazakhstan. Four people in fatigues had penetrated a military facility as slick as could be, then disposed of the arms dealer within spitting distance of a hundred armed troops. A pair of guards spotted them going over the fence and fired off a few rounds, but the quartet got away cleanly.

Thereafter, on an average of once a month, the death squad struck again. Europe. The Middle East. Mexico. South America. The scope of their operations was amazing. At first scrutiny there appeared to be no rhyme or reason to their targets except that each was engaged in illegal activity that directly impacted the United States in one form or another, whether it was a cocaine king in Colombia or an illicit supplier of Saturday-night Specials from Mexico City.

The more Brognola learned, the more he leaned toward this notion the death squad had to be officially sanctioned. How else were they zipping all over the world without arousing suspicion? Someone was intruding on his turf, and he would like to know who.

Then Brognola read the expanded Paris report. In it, and in each report that followed, mention was made of a business card crammed into the mouth of each of the victims. Cards imprinted with the likeness of a large black scorpion.

Brognola sat back and thoughtfully tapped his pen on the desk. A sanctioned unit wouldn't indulge in blatant theatrics. It violated every precept of counterespionage. Secrecy was essential. How odd that for nearly a year the death squad had conducted their strikes by the book, then suddenly changed its modus operandi. It was almost as if they wanted everyone to know they were responsible. But that was ludicrous. They might as well take out an ad in the Yellow Pages.

Brognola scanned the last reports once more. The targets were typical. The locations were scattered far and wide, as usual. The death squad got in and out without leaving a clue to its identity. The only new note was the business cards.

Why a black scorpion? Brognola asked himself. Was it supposed to strike terror into those they eliminated? Hardly. They always left the cards after the fact. What other possible purpose could there be, then? He kept returning to the same conclusion. It was the death squad's way of announcing to the world it had done the job. But why draw attention to themselves? Why court notoriety after a year of complete anonymity? To show off? No one would be that childish.

Getting nowhere, Brognola slapped down his pen and stood. He stepped to a window and stretched to relieve a kink in his back. Sometimes the best method for tackling a problem was to ignore it for a while, then attack it again from a fresh perspective. He gazed out over the nation's capital, currently awash in a light drizzle, and his gaze fell on a distant neon sign above a popular pizza restaurant.

Advertising. Maybe the angle wasn't as far-fetched as he believed. Brognola paced the room, his mind racing. Fact: the death squad had gone public. Corollary: they had to want someone to know they existed. But whom? The answer leaped out at him as vividly as the neon sign.

"I'll be damned," Brognola said and sat back down. Advertising was done for one purpose. To lure in customers. To attract new clients. The business cards were the death squad's way of lining up work. That had to be it. No other explanation made any sense.

The intercom buzzed and Brognola absently answered. "Who is it?"

"Agent Farrow, sir. We've been running a comparative match of the video footage from Perigord Industries with personnel records from every military, law enforcement and government branch, as you requested, and we've found something that will interest you."

"So soon?"

"Sometimes the good guys get lucky, sir."

THE EXECUTIONER ESTIMATED the approaching vehicles were a mile off. More than enough for him to arrange a little surprise for Keefer and company.

"Dayka, where are you?" the cell phone crackled. "Are you still questioning that tramp from the bar? Has the trollop told you anything?"

"Dayka is dead," Bolan said. "So are the others. And your chopper went down in the swamp. You shouldn't send amateurs to do a professional's job."

The silence at the other end was thick enough to cut with a butter knife. "Who is this?" the woman inquired, a trace of amusement in her tone.

"Ladies first."

"Everyone has been calling me Belle for so many years, I've forgotten my real name," the woman bantered. "Now it's your turn."

"I seem to have forgotten my real name, too."

Belle laughed merrily. Her voice had a husky quality

that would make most men fall over themselves to please her. "I think maybe I like you," she said. "How about if we call you Badass? You're one of Carbou's boys, yes?"

"I'm no one's boy, least of all his."

"You can't be police," Belle stated. "They wouldn't send one lone cop on a raid. So you must be government."

The lady was perceptive and uncomfortably close to the truth. "I know who I am," Bolan said. "But where do you fit into the scheme of things? Why isn't Rabican running this operation? Don't tell me you're his second in command?"

"My mother used to have a saying. Never judge others by our own prejudices." Belle's voice acquired a flinty edge. "Are you one of those primitives who think a woman's place is in the home?"

"No, but I've seen Rabican. He doesn't impress me as the liberated type."

Her laughter was infectious. "I like you more and more, Badass. No, Henri isn't the most open-minded of men. But he has his uses."

"Like a pit bull does?"

"*Oui, monsieur.* My compliments on the keenness of your mind. A pity your existence will soon end at the hands of Keefer's men and we will never get to meet. But that is life, eh? We are like flowers. We take seed, we bloom, we fade and we are forgotten. I bid you a most fond *au revoir.*"

The dial tone blared in Bolan's ear. By now he was three-quarters of a mile from the oncoming vehicles. Braking to a stop, he switched off the headlights.

"I shudder to ask what you're up to this time," Nina commented.

Bolan turned and opened the duffel bag. From it he removed a carrying case, and from the case he took a rectangular object about eight and a half inches long by three and three-quarters inches high.

"What in the world is that thing?"

"It's called a Claymore."

"Don't they, like, blow people all to bits?" Nina edged back as if afraid it would go off. "God, next you'll be pulling a cannon out of that magic bag of yours."

"It would make things a whole lot easier if we had one." With the Claymore in one hand, the carrying case in the other, Bolan slid out. "For once will you stay put? I need to rig this."

"Don't worry. My tush isn't leaving this seat."

Bolan moved past the Jeep. He had two choices. He could rig the mine to detonate electrically, or he could set up a trip wire and let the smugglers set it off themselves. He went with the wire. At a point where two saplings flanked the road on either side, he knelt next to the tree on the right and swiftly unfolded the Claymore's scissors-type folding legs. An M-21 vertical penetration mine or an M-19 blast mine would work better. They were specifically designed to take out vehicles. But the Claymore would suffice.

Bolan removed a spool of wire from the carrying case. Unraveling it, he backed toward the tree on the other side of the road and began to loop the wire tight.

Bolan hastened back to the first tree. He slid the primer adapter and a blasting cap from a pouch. A few moments more, and it was time to attach the wire to the Claymore. This was the tricky part. A sudden sneeze, and the smugglers could scoop up his remains with a dustpan. He worked as delicately as a feather, and when he was done, he slowly backed off, the case clasped to his chest.

Only when he turned did Bolan discover the overhead

light inside the Jeep was on. Sprinting over, he slid in. "What the hell are you doing?" They might as well have sent up a flare to show Keefer exactly where they were.

Nina had twisted the rearview mirror and was fiddling with her hair. "What does it look like? I'm a mess. I can't go back into town like this."

Switching off the light, Bolan shoved the carrying case into the rear and started the engine. The oncoming vehicles were still about half a mile off, so there was a chance they hadn't seen the glow. Leaving off the headlights, he threw the vehicle into reverse, twisted so he could see behind them and started to back up.

"Care to fill me in?" Nina requested.

"Claymores have a forward blast radius of close to 750 feet. They also have a back blast to the rear and the sides," Bolan informed her. "Not as far, but we should be at least three hundred feet away when it goes off."

"Did they teach you all this at Hit Man School?"

"Come again?"

"I have it figured out. You're one of those hit men I've seen on TV. You go around whacking people for a living. It explains everything. The guns, the grenades, the frigging mine."

"Nothing gets past you, does it?" Bolan said.

Pleased with herself, Nina smiled. "I might be slow on the uptake, but I'm no dummy. Fact is, I admire you. Some of the men I've been with were real momma's boys. They liked to puff up their chests and act all macho, but they couldn't lick a ten-year-old. You, on the other hand, can lick an army without working up a sweat."

"I wouldn't go that far."

"I had a cousin who was sent into the service," Nina prattled. "The Navy, I think it was. Anyway, he went in there all fired up to blow the hell out of that foreign bozo who is always giving us a hard time. You know the one I mean? Well, the stupid Navy went and made him a cook. Can you believe it?"

If her cousin was anything like her, Bolan could understand why. He liked it better when she was quiet. It hadn't been obvious before, but she was as shallow as a dry creek. Yet rather sweet, in a goofy sort of way.

"I thought about going in the service. But the uniforms they make those women wear are atrocious. I mean, the hems are down to their ankles, and they don't get to show any cleavage. What's up with that?"

Bolan idly wondered if he had a spare sock in his duffel he could use as a gag. He brought the Jeep to a halt, then shifted into first gear and kept his left foot on the clutch. When the time came to move, they had to go fast.

HAL BROGNOLA OPENED THE E-mail Farrow had sent him. The image that appeared on the screen was of a tall, muscular soldier with brown hair and eyes.

"We decided to run a check of military records first," Farrow was saying. "I concentrated on active duty personnel, Jennings on personnel discharged within the past two years. He came up with this."

"Kyle Carson," Brognola read. "Former U.S. Army Airborne Ranger. Served with the First Battalion, Seventy-fifth Regiment. Dishonorably discharged after a training incident in which two soldiers lost their lives." He motioned at Farrow. "I want a complete copy of the court-martial proceedings leading to his discharge."

"Jennings is already on it, sir."

Brognola tapped a key and the screen split in two. On the right was the Ranger photo, on the left a still image taken from the video footage from Perigord Industries.

The man on the left had blond hair and a blond mustache, but there was no denying they were one and the same.

"Bingo."

"There's no current address on file for Carson," Farrow disclosed. "He seems to have disappeared off the face of the earth about eighteen or nineteen months ago."

About the time the death squad made its first hit, Brognola reflected. "Good work. Keep at it, and you'll earn a couple of extra days off to spend with that little girl of yours." Farrow was a single mom doing her best to juggle motherhood and a career.

"Thank you, sir." She whisked from the room.

Brognola studied the two photos, mulling various aspects. Was it safe to assume the members of the death squad were all former military? Or had whoever formed the squad chosen from other branches of government as well? What was the criterion for selecting them? Their individual skills?

The big Fed's brow furrowed. It stood to reason that someone kicked out of the Rangers might hold a grudge against the military and the government in general. Yet Carson had spent the past year and a half putting his life on the line to eliminate enemies of his country. That took exceptional dedication. Could it be, Brognola mused, that the criterion for choosing the death squad members had been their sense of patriotism? Unlikely, since at first glance Carson was an improbable candidate.

The big Fed's phone rang and he lifted the receiver. "Brognola here."

"Ike Mathews, DEA. You called me three days ago, remember?"

Mathews was handling the Drug Enforcement Administration's efforts to cap the flow of illegal drugs into southern Louisiana. Brognola had requested a breakdown of the agency's current operations to avoid potential conflicts when Bolan went in. Wherever possible, he liked to avoid stepping on other agencies' toes. Swiveling his chair away from the computer, Brognola propped a foot on the edge of his desk. He had been cooped up in his office too long. He needed to get out and stretch his legs. "Certainly, Agent Mathews."

"You asked me to keep you posted on new developments. And the strangest thing has happened."

Brognola figured Mathews had heard about the firefight at the salt dome. The DEA had a couple of snitches they were milking, midlevel flunkies, one of whom had fed them the tip about the latest shipment due in. "I'm all ears."

"The word on the street is that there was a hit on Rabican."

"Oh?" Brognola tried to sound surprised, but he wasn't much of an actor. "Did it succeed?"

"No. I sent out feelers to confirm Carbou was behind it. And the word I got back is that Carbou has hired outsiders to whack Rabican. Professionals with a long string of hits to their credit."

Brognola's pulse quickened. Lowering his foot to the floor, he sat up straight. "You don't say? Any word on who these outsiders are?"

"Not much, no. Carbou is playing it very close to the vest. I guess he doesn't want it to become common knowledge he couldn't take down Rabican on his own."

"Oh." Brognola's disappointment knew no bounds.

"The only tidbit we've gleaned is that these outsiders call themselves the Scorpions. Our snitch claims they'll whack anyone for four hundred thousand per hit." Mathews paused. "Ever heard of them?"

Brognola felt like whooping for joy. The calling cards Carson and his friends had been leaving now made perfect sense. It was publicity, the kind only word of mouth in the right circles could spread. They were getting the word out that they were available. He had been right. It *was* advertising.

"Mr. Brognola, are you still there?"

"I sure am," Brognola responded. "And I can't thank you enough for the call. I'll get back to you shortly with more information. In the meantime, continue to have your people keep a low profile. If anything else pops up on your end, let me know."

MADELINE CULVER WAS PACING the living room of her apartment when the knock sounded. She checked who it was through the peephole before working the dead bolt and undoing the three extra locks she had installed. "Get in here," she said, yanking on her visitor's sleeve. "Tell me how it went."

Rico Fuentes gave her place the once-over and his mouth curled in disdain. "I still don't see why you stay in this dump. All the money we've made so far, you could set yourself up in style."

"It's called keeping a low profile," Culver said. "Something you would do well to remember." Folding her arms, she impatiently waited. "Well?"

"How do you think it went?" Fuentes responded. "He was candy. I untied him and left the body lying in the tub. It will look like an accident. He slipped, hit his head and drowned. Poor Mr. Considine."

"Did you remember to take whatever you tied him with and wipe everything else clean of prints?"

Fuentes sniffed in mild indignation. "What do you take me for? There's nothing to link me to the scene."

The Gold Eagle Reader Service™ — Here's how it works:

If offer card is missing write to: Gold Eagle Reader Service, 3010 Walden Ave., P.O. Box 1867, Buffalo, NY 14240-1867

NO POSTAGE
NECESSARY
IF MAILED
IN THE
UNITED STATES

BUSINESS REPLY MAIL
FIRST-CLASS MAIL   PERMIT NO. 717-003   BUFFALO, NY

POSTAGE WILL BE PAID BY ADDRESSEE

GOLD EAGLE READER SERVICE
3010 WALDEN AVE
PO BOX 1867
BUFFALO NY 14240-9952

GET FREE BOOKS and a FREE GIFT WHEN YOU PLAY THE...

Lucky 7

SLOT MACHINE GAME!

Just scratch off the silver box with a coin. Then check below to see the gifts you get!

YES!

I have scratched off the silver box. Please send me the 2 free Gold Eagle® books and gift for which I qualify. I understand I am under no obligation to purchase any books, as explained on the back of this card.

366 ADL DRSG   **166 ADL DRSF**

FIRST NAME   LAST NAME

ADDRESS

APT.#   CITY

STATE/PROV.   ZIP/POSTAL CODE

7	7	7
🍒	🍒	🍒
♣	♣	♣
🔔	🔔	🍒

Worth TWO FREE BOOKS plus a BONUS Mystery Gift!

Worth TWO FREE BOOKS!

Worth ONE FREE BOOK!

TRY AGAIN!

(MB-01/03)

DETACH AND MAIL CARD TODAY!

"There had better not be," she warned, "because if they bag you, they might persuade you to cop a deal and turn the rest of us in for a lighter sentence."

"I would never betray you," Fuentes promised.

Culver's chuckle was as brittle as North Pole ice. "If you're saying I should trust you, Rico, forget it. The only person I trust is myself."

Rico nodded toward her bedroom. "Does that apply to him as well?"

"My personal life isn't open to discussion." Culver opened the door wide enough to verify the hallway was empty. "Off you go. Remember, we're leaving at six for Baton Rouge, and this time we'll get the damn job done right."

"We were bound to blow one eventually," Fuentes mentioned. "Too bad. Carbou wasn't happy Rabican got away."

"Can you blame him? We promised and we didn't deliver. Unless we make good, you can forget retiring in a couple of years to a life of bikini-clad babes. No one will want to hire us."

Fuentes slipped past. "Catch you on the flip side, Maddy."

Culver threw the bolt and secured the locks. As she worked the last one a slight noise caused her to stiffen slightly. "I thought you were asleep, lover," she said and turned.

Kyle Carson, clad in boxers, was leaning against the jamb to her bedroom doorway. "You did it anyway. After I asked you not to."

Shrugging, she crossed to the sofa and threw herself onto her back. "You heard Considine at the restaurant. There was no reasoning with the man. It was his way or the highway, and I, for one, wasn't about to pass up a once-in-a-lifetime opportunity to become a millionaire."

"That's all that matters to you, isn't it? The money?"

Culver stifled a laugh. Of the four of them, he was the most naive, the most trusting. Enticing him into her boudoir had been ridiculously easy. Now he was hers to manipulate as she saw fit. "I keep forgetting you were raised on a farm, and your parents instilled all those old-fashioned values in you."

"We betrayed him, Maddy. There's no glossing over it."

"It was him or us. When will you get that through your thick Nebraskan skull?" Culver drummed her fingers on a cushion. "I'm trying to be patient with you, Kyle. I honestly am. But you make it awful hard."

"I gave him my word."

The woman balled a fist in impotent anger. "So what? He was using us to further his career. We were nothing more than cannon fodder."

"He said we were helping our country. He said he was giving us a new lease on life."

"Who are you going to believe, him or me?" Culver mentally counted to ten before going on. Softening her tone, she smiled and crooked a finger. "Come on over here and let ol' Maddy massage those big shoulders of yours. You need to learn to take things in stride, lover. Everything will work out. You'll see." She had it all planned. They had agreed to disband the Scorpions when they each had a million cached away. But to her way of thinking, two million was better than one million, and four million was better than two. Her partners didn't know it yet, but their retirements would be literal and permanent. Carson first, then the others.

He walked over, sat next to her and stroked her cheek. "You're so beautiful. Sometimes I can't believe you really care as much as you do."

"There's no one I love more," Culver said, which was true as far as it went. Excluding herself, naturally. Looping her arms around his neck, she pulled him down on top of her. "Never forget, handsome. I always know best."

Headlights mushroomed around a curve and bore down on the Jeep containing the Executioner and the woman fate had temporarily thrust into his care.

"We're just going to sit here?" Nina anxiously inquired. "In another half a minute they'll spot us."

"In another half a minute I'll want them to." Bolan had one hand on the headlight knob. He was waiting for the smugglers to reach the right spot. From what he could tell, the vehicles were four-wheel drives, Blazers or Broncos or something similar. Their beams splayed steadily closer.

"I hope you know what you're doing."

They were about to find out. Bolan twisted the knob and the Jeep's headlights speared toward the trucks. It had the desired effect. The lead vehicle slowed. And the slower it was moving, the more damage the Claymore would do.

A few seconds later the lead truck hit the trigger wire.

A roiling blast of blistering force ripped into the Blazer and reduced much of it to a twisted mass of tangled metal. The front end reared up off the ground and it lurched toward the left side of the road, flames and smoke gusting from what was left of the engine.

"Roll down your window, then duck," Bolan commanded, then popped the clutch. The Jeep shot toward the remaining four-wheel-drive vehicle, which had slanted to the right and screeched to a stop.

Not knowing what had caused the explosion and thinking they would be targeted next, triggermen were spilling from all four doors and taking cover.

Nina frantically cranked her window. She saw Bolan take hold of the M-16, and she bent below the dash even though she had the window only halfway down.

It was enough. The Executioner rested the sound suppressor on the upper edge. As the Jeep sped past the second vehicle, he peppered its tires. The gunners returned fire but not with any precision. A few rounds pinged off the front fender. Others cored the roof. Then the Jeep rapidly accelerated.

"Is it safe?" Nina inquired a minute later. She timidly raised her head high enough to look behind them. "I'll be damned. You did it again. Now all you have to do is get me to my apartment so I can pick up a few things, take me to the bus depot and I'll be out of your hair."

"Is that all?" Bolan said dryly.

"Well, you did say you could help me out financially."

They hadn't gone a mile when the same cell phone beeped. Bolan pressed the button to answer it, but didn't say anything.

Throaty laughter broke a short interval of silence. "What am I going to do about you, Badass?" Belle asked. "I just got a call from Keefer. He says you turned half his men into gator bait and put both his trucks out of commission."

"I'm going to do the same to your pit bull," Bolan said.

"My poor Rabican. So many mongrels want to rip out his throat." Belle made a *tsk-tsk* sound. "By the way, I know who you are now. One of those hired killers. What is it you call yourselves? Oh, yes. The Scorpions."

"Never heard of them."

Belle started to laugh, then sensed he was serious. "You're not a Scorpion? I am confused. Perhaps I should— what is the expression?—dig a hole and crawl into it until this insanity is over."

Bolan was a keen judge of human nature. He had to be. Frequently, first impressions meant the difference between life and death. And his first impression of the woman at the other end was of a piranha in female guise. Accordingly he remarked, "You're not the type to run and hide."

"Most discerning of you. I am always most dangerous when I am cornered. So be careful. You and these Scorpions, you will all regret interfering in our business." She hung up.

Switching off the phone, Bolan slid it into a pouch and settled back for the long drive into Baton Rouge. The night's events had taken a toll on Nina, and she was soon sound asleep. He decided to place a call to Brognola, but he didn't use the phone from the landscaping company or the phone he had found in the Jeep. The Feds could subpoena the cellular companies who supplied them and obtain a complete record of every call ever placed. It might raise eyebrows if the big Fed's number showed up. So he used his own.

"Brognola here."

"You're up late."

"We've had a major break at this end," Brognola said excitedly. "Those four people you thought were DEA, the ones from the salt dome, they're a death squad, but with a difference. They hire themselves out for almost half a mil per hit. And you'll never guess what they call themselves."

"The Scorpions."

The big Fed was quiet for an unusually long time. "You know, Striker, just once I'd like to be able to surprise you. Keep this up and you'll give me a complex. How in hell did you learn who they were?"

Succinctly Bolan explained, ending with, "Find out what you can about Belle. I have a gut feeling there's more to her than just being Rabican's woman."

"This whole situation has become too complicated for my liking," Brognola remarked. "We have Rabican and his boys on one side, Carbou and his goons on the other and a wild card, the Scorpions. Any one of whom will kill you without a second thought."

Bolan recalled the soldier at the salt dome who had tried to spare him from possible harm. "It's not as if I haven't been in situations like this before."

"At times like this I wish you'd accept some backup. How about if I make a call to Stony Man and see who's available? Jack had been complaining that all he does is fly lately. I'm sure he wouldn't mind getting out in the field." The big Fed was referring to Jack Grimaldi, Stony Man Farm's ace pilot.

"No."

"How about Gary Manning or David McCarter? They can't stand twiddling their thumbs for long, and it's been a couple of weeks since Phoenix Force saw action."

"I'm fine, Mother."

The big Fed indulged in some rare profanity.

"I'll call you this evening." Bolan ignored the barbs. "If you have to reach me before then, phone me at the motel." He checked his watch, calculated the driving time to Baton

Rouge, the time it would take Nina to pack, and allowed for the ride to the bus terminal. "I should be back in my room by eight a.m. at the latest."

"Before you go, tell me more about this lady friend of yours. Nina, isn't it? Jack will have a cow when he hears you're picking up hookers."

Bolan ended the call and grinned.

THE SCORPIONS BOOKED commercial flights. As was their custom, Culver and Carson took one, Fuentes and Placer another. They traveled under false identities, thanks to their recently deceased handler, and each possessed several driver's licenses, social security cards and passports.

Culver's seat was seven rows in front of Carson's. They deliberately avoided talking to each other. When they disembarked, the woman went straight to a rental car booth while Carson followed at discreet distance, pretending to be interested in a magazine. It was his job to determine if they were being shadowed. Not until he was convinced it was safe did he signal to Culver before going to the front of the terminal to wait for her to pick him up. From the airport they drove to a Holiday Inn.

Fuentes and Placer wouldn't arrive for two hours. Culver used the time to buy hair dye and turn herself into a brunette. At her insistence, Carson changed his black hair to a sandy color. When he came out of the bathroom she was bent over the bed, studying a map.

"Tonight we'll nail Rabican for sure, lover," Culver declared, tapping the map. "Now that we know where his lair is."

"You trust Carbou?"

"Hell no. But I trust his information. He wants his money's worth. He wouldn't provide bogus intel."

"And once we've eliminated Rabican, what then?"

"We stick to the master plan. We keep selling our services until each of us has a cool million in the bank."

"Without Considine and his contacts, it's going to be harder."

"*Au contraire,* handsome," she rebutted. "I have a copy of his files, including all the lists he made of targets for us to hit. There must be hundreds. Only from our point of view, they're potential clients." She chuckled and winked.

"What about ammo, gear, clothes and plane rides?" Carson said. "We relied on him for all of those, remember?"

"Plane rides are why travel agencies were invented. Civvies we can get at any shopping mall. There are military outlets all over the country that sell combat fatigues and general equipment. As for ammo and the specialized stuff, we'll have to find contacts on the black market."

Carson stared at her, his face inscrutable. "You have an answer for everything."

"No, I just planned ahead." Culver sat on the bed, one knee crooked. "What is with you today, anyway? Stop moping about Considine. He's not the martyr you make him out to be. All that bull about duty to God and country was a scam to get us to do his dirty work. I never fell for it for a minute, and I'm amazed you did."

"I believe in this country, Maddy. I enlisted in the Army to do my part."

"And what did they do? They booted you out over something that wasn't even your fault. Was that the thanks you deserved?"

"I don't blame the Army for that," Carson replied. "It was the general, Private Wilson's father, who pushed to have me thrown out. I can't really blame him, either. He lost a son he loved very much."

Rather sadly, Culver shook her head. "You're a throw-back, Kyle. You belong to an earlier age, to a time when people were decent and cared about their fellow man. Look around you. Times have changed. Selfishness is in. It's every person for himself."

"Sometimes I wonder why I love you so much."

Culver blinked and came off the bed to embrace him. "I worry when you talk like that." She kissed him full on the lips. "We were destined to be together. It was love at first sight." She caressed his cheek. "I need you to stay focused, Kyle. We can't afford slipups out in the field. I cover your back, you cover mine. Isn't that what we agreed?"

Carson nodded but without much enthusiasm.

"Look, whenever you start to feel all sentimental and sappy, remember the money. All that wonderful, glorious money. More than any of us have ever seen. Anything you've ever wanted will be yours."

"All I want is you."

For a few moments she didn't react. Then she smiled and traced his square chin with the tip of a finger. "Damn me if you're not serious. No one has ever cared for me as much as you. It's flattering, but it's also troubling."

"Troubling how?" the tall soldier asked.

"You're like a puppy, lover. A great big adorable puppy. The kind people want to pick up, cuddle and take home."

"What's wrong with that?"

"You're a soldier. You're supposed to be a lean, mean fighting machine. A wolf, not a puppy. Try to remember that. We have a long, tough road ahead of us, and I want you with me when we reach the end." Culver kissed him, and he closed his eyes and melted against her. She wanted him to live, true enough, so he would have that much more money for her to take for her own. And it helped to have one person on the team she could trust. A year from now, when he had outlived his usefulness, she would close those puppy eyes of his for good.

CYPRESS TREES LINED the road, their branches draped with Spanish moss. A legion of crickets droned an insect chorus, while overhead sparkled a myriad of stars. Bolan downshifted to take a tight turn, driving the Jeep deeper into thickly forested country north of Baton Rouge.

Hal Brognola had come through for him once again. The big Fed had identified the woman who called herself Belle as one Blanche Dalcour. Born and raised on a hardscrabble farm by an alcoholic father and a Cajun mother, she fled to New Orleans when she was sixteen. On her own, with no skills and no income, she ended up behind bars when a john she solicited refused to meet her price and she slashed him with a knife. The judge took pity on her because of her youth, and she received a light sentence. Four years later she was arrested again for peddling stolen merchandise. A savvy lawyer got her off, but the local law was watching her closely so she pulled up stakes and moved to Baton Rouge. As near as the Feds could tell, that was where she met Rabican and about the same time changed her name.

"She's a shrewd one." Brognola had said by way of a compliment. "If not for you, we wouldn't know where to find her."

By that, Brognola was referring to the pair of cell phones Bolan had obtained. On his arrival at the motel that morning, the soldier had been met by a pair of federal agents sent to get them. It didn't take the Feds long to track down the local telecommunications firms that supplied the phones. One was to a business account, Canbiar Landscaping, Incorporated. The other user was Anton

Chipouque, otherwise known as Chippy, a low-level cog in Rabican's organization.

The phone records were still being examined. But already the Feds had established that dozens of calls were made from the landscaping company to a certain residence northwest of Baton Rouge, an estate belonging to one Morgana Plaquemine, which just happened to be the maiden name of Belle's mother.

Bolan was on his way to check it out. Brognola had offered to send in his people, but Bolan elected to do it himself. He'd had a solid eight hours sleep and was well rested. After wolfing a supper of burgers and fries from a fast-food outlet, he hopped in the Jeep and headed out. Now he was miles from Baton Rouge, on the lookout for an oxbow lake and the mansion that bordered it. Oxbow lakes were fairly common west of the Mississippi. Evidently they had once been curves in rivers long since cut off from main waterways.

As he drove, Bolan mulled over the other intel Brognola had imparted.

A second Scorpion had been identified. Acting on the assumption some of the others might be former military, like Sergeant Kyle Carson, Brognola had his people do a rundown of personnel dishonorably discharged in the past five years. They hit pay dirt. Another image from the Perigord footage was matched to the photo ID of Corporal Rico Fuentes, a former Marine who had disgraced the corps.

The Feds had every reason to believe the Scorpions were still in Louisiana, and Bolan agreed. The death squad was being paid big bucks to kill Henri Rabican, and they weren't about to quit until the job was done.

There was still no word on the mastermind behind the Scorpions. Brognola was of the opinion it had to be someone with access to restricted government records, someone with extensive contacts, someone who knew how to pull the necessary strings to outfit the Scorpions and see to their travel needs. "That takes a lot of paperwork," Brognola had mentioned. "Official forms and whatnot. Which means they've left a paper trail that will lead us right to their leader."

"You don't think it's one of the Scorpions?" Bolan had asked.

"Not judging by Carson and Fuentes, no. Former grunts couldn't set up an operation of this complexity and scope. Fuentes barely made it through the tenth grade. And Carson just doesn't strike me as the type."

"How do you mean?"

"I've read the transcript of his court-martial. It was a snow job. He was railroaded out of the Army. And it's too bad, because his service record indicates he was an exemplary soldier. Hard working. Dedicated. With a fine career ahead of him if it hadn't been for those chutes fouling." Brognola sighed. "Carson just doesn't fit the psych profile of a rogue. I don't understand why he hooked up with them."

"I'll ask him next time I see him."

"Look, I know you think he had your best interests at heart at the salt dome, but you don't know that for sure. He was a good soldier once, I'll admit. But he's gone sour in a big way. So don't let down your guard if you meet up with him again."

Bolan rounded another turn and slowed for four does crossing the road. The strong fragrance of honeysuckle wafted from the nearby woods, and he heard a wildcat screech in the distance.

The road climbed to the brow of a hill that afforded

Bolan a panoramic vista of the terrain ahead. He spied the glistening surface of a crescent-shaped lake. On its north shore, bathed in light, was an antebellum-style mansion and half a dozen outbuildings. Cars lined a circular driveway, and there appeared to be a lot of activity centered around a barn or stable.

Bolan descended the hill and drove midway along the mile-long lake. On the left the forest was broken by a field. Pulling off, he parked well back from the road. From his duffel he selected a Kevlar vest and shrugged into it. Next, out came the Desert Eagle, his M-16 and several grenades. The Beretta, as always, went into the shoulder rig. Lastly he applied combat cosmetics to his face and neck, strapped a compass to his right wrist and climbed out of the vehicle.

A car approached from the north. Rock music blared, and it swept by, a girl's high-pitched laughter trailing after it.

Bolan jogged to the other side and on through dense undergrowth to the lake. As he stepped onto its shore, a brown pelican rose into the air with startled flapping. Once above the trees, it circled, then flew south.

The soldier was too far from the mansion for anyone to have noticed. Hugging vegetation, he glided toward the house. Out on the lake a fish jumped with a loud splash. He glanced toward the sound and was glad he did.

Someone was out there in a boat. Dropping into a crouch, Bolan brought the Raptor scope to bear. Two elderly men in a small rowboat were quietly fishing. They hadn't seen him. He warily moved on, never once exposing himself to their view.

The shoreline curved to form the northwest tip of the crescent. Beyond, to the north, stood the mansion. People were moving about on a wide portico, but nowhere near as many as were busy at the stable. Two diesel trucks with long silver trailers had been backed up to wide double doors and were being loaded by a large work crew.

Kneeling, Bolan surveyed the layout with an eye to infiltrating the mansion. Hedges and flower gardens decorated a spacious lawn, and would provide plenty of cover. Azalea bushes grew along two sides of the portico. From there, all he had to do was find a door or unlatched window.

Bolan rose and quick-stepped to within fifty feet of the driveway. The cars were parked bumper to bumper. He considered jotting down the license plate numbers for the Feds but deemed the risk too great. Eliminating Rabican was more important. No one challenged him as he sprinted to a hedge and squatted. Conversations from the stable were loud enough to overhear, but many of the workers were Cajuns, and spoke in their rapid-fire mix of French and English. A translator would come in handy.

Hunching, Bolan moved along the hedge toward the center of the yard. He hadn't gone more than a dozen feet when the acrid odor of cigarette smoke warned him he wasn't alone. Rising, he peered over the top of the hedge.

A lone guard patrolled the next aisle, the tip of a cigarette glowing red in the darkness.

Tucking at the knees, Bolan shadowed him. He walked at the same pace, stopped when the guard stopped. The man clearly wasn't expecting intruders and acted half-bored.

Bolan spotted a gap in the hedge up ahead. Dropping to his stomach, he made himself as inconspicuous as he could.

The guard ambled through the gap, an Armalite AR-18

slung over one shoulder. He yawned, then turned left, away from Bolan. Soon he blended into the darkness.

Thick grass muffled the tread of Bolan's shoes as he proceeded to the gap and through to the next hedgerow. Other gaps, staggered at irregular intervals, brought him to a flower garden bristling with rose bushes and gardenias. Crawling in among them, Bolan found a vantage point from which he could see both the mansion and the stable. Bright floodlights made using the scope unnecessary, so he switched off the night-vision.

From where he lay, Bolan discovered a third unmarked tractor trailer had been backed up to the south side of the mansion. A ramp had been lowered and workers in overalls were loading furniture and other household items. Rabican had to suspect his enemies were closing in so he was clearing out. The smuggler hadn't lasted as long as he had by being stupid. By morning everyone and everything would be long gone.

Bolan studied the people on the portico. Four women and five men were seated around circular white tables, drinking and chatting. None was Rabican. Bolan studied the mansion windows one by one. Most were ablaze with light, and every so often he saw workers move back and forth, cleaning out the rooms.

The growl of a powerful engine heralded the arrival of a Corvette. It pulled up to the marble steps and out hopped someone in a three-piece suit.

It took a few seconds for Bolan to recognize the dapper figure as the one he was after. He brought the M-16 to bear, but by then Rabican had bounded up the steps and the men and women on the portico were gathering around to greet him. He couldn't get a clear shot.

Bolan refused to fire indiscriminately. Granted, the

women might belong to the smuggler's network, but then again, they might not. He watched the group move indoors. Over the course of the next half hour, he never took his eyes off the windows. He entertained the hope Rabican would show himself, but the smuggler never did. Meanwhile, the workers continued to fill the trailer, and the men at the stable continued to load up whatever was stored there.

Bolan crossed his arms in front of him and rested his chin on his wrist. He had all night to wait. With so much going on, eventually Rabican would reappear. One shot, and Lafe Carbou would find himself the king of Louisiana's smugglers. A short-lived reign, since Carbou was next on his list.

An hour dragged by. Two hours.

The soldier looked up when a commotion occurred at the stable. Men were shouting. The ramps were being raised. Drivers were climbing into the truck cabs. Pulsing diesel engines throbbed to life, more yells were exchanged, and the big rigs rumbled down the drive in tandem, turning south.

Bolan had the rifle tucked to his shoulder. He expected Rabican to show himself, but no such luck. The trucks vanished into the distance. Some of the men who had helped load them piled into vehicles and departed. The rest entered the mansion.

Resigning himself to a longer wait, Bolan lowered the M-16. A large beetle scooted across his hand. A mosquito buzzed his left ear. He didn't so much as blink. But he did react when the front door opened and out walked a lovely blonde attired in an elaborate blue evening dress. She came to the top of the marble steps, gazed out over the estate, then clasped her slim hands behind her thin waist and slowly descended. At the bottom she did exactly the thing Bolan didn't want her to do.

She came straight toward the flower garden.

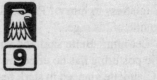

9

The Executioner froze. Discovery would ruin everything. Gunners would converge from all directions, and in the confusion Rabican might get away.

The woman had a sorrowful air about her. She was in her mid-to-late thirties, and extremely attractive. Ruby lips, rosy cheeks and a lustrous sheen to her hair were enough to turns male heads. She also had an hourglass body, the kind most women dreamed about. Walking up to the roses, she bent and sniffed one not six feet from Bolan's position. "I will miss you," she said softly.

Her sultry voice told Bolan it was the woman who called herself Belle. To say she was nothing like he expected was an understatement. He caught the scent of exotic, musky perfume, and felt a stirring.

Belle carefully plucked the rose and gently held it in

both hands. "How tragic. So beautiful and fragile one day, withered and rotting the next."

The front door opened again. A younger woman in a maid's uniform scanned the yard, spotted Belle and skipped down the steps two at a time. "Madam! Madam! You must come at once."

"What is it now, Claudette?" Belle asked with a weariness beyond her years.

"He is asking for you. He is drinking, too, and you know how he gets when he drinks." Claudette motioned for her mistress to hurry. "Please. Let's go in before he flies into one of his rages."

"Let him," Belle said and sniffed the rose again. "His male posturing has no effect on me. I will do as I please."

Claudette glanced in stark fear at the mansion. "Please, Madam! Don't let him hear you talk like that."

"Or what? He'll lift a hand against me? Let him try just once. He knows I would leave him, and he cannot live without me." Belle held out the rose. "To him I am more precious than this exquisite flower."

"I beg of you, Madam. I am only doing what he ordered me to do. I cannot afford to lose my job."

"I give you my word you won't be fired," Belle assured her. "Now run inside and inform his lordship I will be along shortly." She wagged her hand and the maid hastened toward the steps.

Suddenly a tremendous blast shattered the night and a section of the west wall was blown outward, leaving a gaping cavity. Autofire burst from different points of the compass and shouts broke out both inside and outside the mansion.

"My God!" Claudette exclaimed. "What's happening?"

"We are under attack."

Guns were booming; SMGs chattered. One of Rabican's underlings broke a window on the third floor and craned his head out. "I don't see anyone!" he shouted.

Somewhere near the stable a sound-suppressed weapon fired and the simpleton sprawled over the sill.

"We must get inside, Madam!" Claudette ran to her mistress and gripped her arm. "Come now!"

But Belle didn't move. She stayed in the shadows and calmly whispered, "We're safer here. Don't make a sound."

"The men will protect us!" Claudette cried and rushed to the marble steps. She wasn't quite midway up them when the sniper by the stable spotted her and his weapon fired several times. Crimson dots speckled her uniform, and she was flung onto her face.

Belle took a step, then drew up short. The serenity that lined her features earlier was gone. Sheer savagery claimed her, from her bared teeth to her clenched fists and bowstring posture. She had been transformed from a genteel lady of leisure into the embodiment of vengeance.

Bolan was listening to the bedlam. He had a knack for isolating and identifying individual weapons by their characteristic sounds, and it told him the mansion was under fire from the north, the east and the west. But only three attackers were involved. The initial blast had been a grenade, for shock effect more than anything else. Now they were keeping the occupants pinned down.

The front door was flung wide and out rushed two of Rabican's men. They raced to the top step and one bellowed, "Belle? Belle? Where are you?" One of them saw the maid and bounded toward her crumpled form.

Belle hadn't answered. She either was playing it safe by not advertising her location, or she had uncanny intuition. As the gunner reached the maid and bent to roll her over, an SMG barked. Not from the north, east or west this time, but instead from the south, from the hedgerows behind Bolan. Precise bursts chopped down both men where they stood. One fell across the maid, the other bounced and slid to the bottom step, his arms and legs akimbo.

Belle whirled and crouched low. Bolan read no fear in her face, just the same grim defiance. She took a couple of steps, trying to pinpoint the fourth shooter. A small mistake, but enough of one that the SMG barked again and she clutched at her shoulder and fell.

Bolan twisted. A shadow had risen from among the hedges and was threading along the rows to the gap that opened onto the garden. The attacker's intention was plain—to finish off Belle.

Lunging out of the rosebushes, Bolan triggered a half-dozen rounds, and the attacker went to ground. A long leap carried him to Belle's side, and he looped his left arm around her waist.

Belle didn't resist or ask who he was. One hand pressed to her wound, she regarded him with fiercely intelligent eyes.

"I'll get you out of here," Bolan said and propelled them across the lawn toward the northwest end of the lake.

Belle's eyes never left his face. She had gone limp so it would be easier for him to bear her weight. Not that she weighed much.

Bolan ran hunched over, anticipating a hail of lead. But they reached the tall weeds along the lake without drawing fire.

"How bad are you hit?" Bolan whispered, setting her down.

"I'll live."

The firefight was reaching a crescendo. Gunners at

nearly every window were firing wildly into the dark. All they were doing was wasting lead and providing backlit targets for the four attackers.

Bolan figured it had to be the Scorpions. They had failed at the salt dome and were out to finish what they started.

"Rabican is a fool," Belle said bitterly.

Bolan agreed. The smuggler should make a break for it while he still could. He had enough men, enough firepower. It hadn't dawned on him the Scorpions were keeping him pinned down for a reason, or what that reason might be.

Belle sat straighter, her wound momentarily forgotten. "What do you think? How will they do it? Explosives in staged charges?"

"How is it you know so much about commando tactics?" Bolan asked.

Her answer was drowned out by four explosions that rocked the adjacent countryside. One after the other, in crashing cadence, the four corners of the mansion were ripped asunder by five or six pounds of what Bolan judged to be C-4. Timed to detonate within seconds of one another, they had the combined effect of lifting the mansion off its foundation and bringing it crashing down in on top of itself. Sturdy stucco walls buckled like plasterboard. The massive beams that supported the upper floors were snapped like sticks. In cinematic slow motion the mansion collapsed, one floor on top of another in pancake fashion. Horrendous screams and nerve-jangling shrieks accompanied the destruction.

Then the upheaval ended. A gigantic cloud of dust hovered over the debris. Parts of the mansion still stood, but they, too, were about to collapse. Wailing and sobbing drifted on the breeze.

"The only real home I ever had," Belle said and bowed her head.

Bolan saw people moving. Many stumbled in shock and confusion, many more were hurt. Some were crawling and crying out for help. Suddenly sound-suppressed autofire raked the scene. The Scorpions were mowing down those still alive. Men and women alike were riddled in their tracks. Some tried to run, but there was nowhere to hide. The Scorpions had them in a withering cross fire.

Belle's head jerked up and she pushed erect. "No!" She started to push through the weeds. "I can't let that happen!"

Bolan grabbed her and held on. "There's nothing you can do. You'll only get yourself killed."

"But I can't just stand here and watch them die!" Belle protested. "Those are my people. They work for me. They trust me. They expect me to do what is right by them." She motioned with her good arm. "Please. You've got a weapon. Do something!"

The Executioner took a step past her, hiked the M-16 to his shoulder and activated the scope. The Scorpions were still pouring lead into the helpless victims from four quarters. He scanned the hedgerows but couldn't spot the Scorpion hidden there. Pivoting, he sought the Scorpion at the stable and this time had better luck. Above the wide main doors was another, much smaller door, an entry to a hayloft. And jutting from it was the business end of a sound suppressor.

The range was beyond the M-16's recommended limit, but Bolan had learned from practical experience that firearms could exceed their specifications in the hands of a skilled shooter. He raised the barrel to allow for the distance, relied on his best judgment to compensate for wind and the slight difference in elevation, sucked in a breath to steady his aim, and triggered a short burst. Quickly he focused the scope on the hayloft door to see if he had come close. Several holes confirmed he had. That, and the sound suppresser had been jerked from sight.

Belle whistled softly in appreciation. "Magnificent! Not many men can shoot like that." Her intense eyes bored into his. "Let me guess. You are not one of the Scorpions. And you're not one of Carbou's men. So you must be Badass, yes?"

Bolan tore his gaze away. She had a rare quality about her, a combination of personal magnetism and sensual presence that bordered on hypnotic allure.

Just then the Scorpion concealed among the hedgerows cut loose again—but not at the survivors of the explosion. The rounds were directed at the tall weeds screening Bolan and the woman. Stems close to the Executioner's elbow were sheared in two. Instinctively he threw himself backward, pulling Belle along with him. He couldn't afford to be gentle, but he tried to cushion the fall by holding her against his chest. He landed on his back with her on top, the tip of her nose touching his, her warm breath fanning his mouth. Her perfume was downright intoxicating. "Sorry," he said, thinking of her wounded shoulder.

A knowing smile curled Belle's lips. "That's quite all right. A man does what a man has to do, eh?"

Bolan rolled onto his side and she slid onto hers, her bosom flush against him, her thighs against his. It took every ounce of willpower he possessed to contain the impulses that rippled through him, and sit up. "We can't stay here," he whispered.

"Take me where you will," Belle responded, wearing an impish grin. "I am yours to command, Badass."

She was one dangerous woman. Bolan rose into a

crouch and helped her off the ground. Parting the weeds, he began to retrace the route he had taken to get there.

The Scorpions had stopped firing for a lack of targets. The people who survived the explosions had been shot down, and not a living soul was moving.

Bolan's lapse appalled him. He prided himself on his self-control, on never losing his focus in combat. Long ago he had learned how to compartmentalize his emotions and personal thoughts so they never intruded when he was on a mission. Yet there was something about Belle that threatened to bring his inner walls tumbling down.

Bolan was the first to admit he was only human. He couldn't expect to function like a robot. There were bound to be instances when his will weakened, however briefly. Still, it was upsetting when it happened because it showed that for all his training and experience, he was prone to the same weaknesses as everyone else. He liked to think he wasn't.

The Executioner cleared his mind of all distracting thoughts. He was a soldier and he would act like one. The weeds ended, and they moved along the lakeshore, staying close to the vegetation as he had done before. The boat with the elderly fishermen had disappeared. He figured they had gone to call the sheriff. It wouldn't be long before deputies arrived, and it was best if he wasn't there.

Bolan glanced over a shoulder to check on how Belle was holding up. She had her hand pressed to the wound and she was breathing heavily, but she hadn't fallen behind. "Once we're safely out of here, I'll bandage you up."

"It is a scrape, nothing more."

Bolan was going to point out that any wound, however minor, entailed the danger of infection, but movement a couple of hundred yards to their rear stilled his tongue. He snapped the scope to his right eye, and the short hairs at his nape prickled as if he had heat rash. Gripping Belle's wrist, he whispered, "They're after us."

"The Scorpions?"

Bolan nodded and ran. The four hired assassins were coming fast, spread out in a skirmish line. Alone, he wouldn't think twice about confronting them. But he had Belle to consider. He told himself she was important to the Feds. He assured himself that Brognola would want to quiz her about her involvement in Rabican's smuggling operation, and maybe try to get her to turn state's evidence in exchange for her help in nailing Carbou. That was why he had to try his best to keep her alive.

The Scorpions wouldn't be easy to shake. They weren't run-of-the-mill triggermen. They were seasoned pros with more kills to their credit than most combat platoons. And they were outfitted with state-of-the-art arms and gear.

Bolan had to decide whether to continue along the shore or cut directly overland to the road. He opted for the former. They could travel faster, for one thing, and a lot more quietly, for another. In her long lacy dress, Belle would make a lot of noise going through the forest.

"They're gaining," the beauty whispered.

The Scorpions were coming on at a full sprint. Of the four, the fleetest was the slenderest. It had to be their leader, the woman who had mowed down Rabican's men at the salt dome and had now masterminded the sweeping assault on the mansion. She liked to pull the trigger.

"We should spring an ambush," Belle proposed, slowing. "Find a spot and take them by surprise."

Bolan tugged to keep her moving. Against ordinary hardmen it might work, but the Scorpions weren't likely to fall for such a basic ruse. Some were bound to have night-vision scopes of their own.

"I owe them for what they did to my people," Belle said angrily. "You can't deny me the right to turn them into maggot bait."

In one respect, Bolan mused, she and the leader of the Scorpions were a lot alike. They were both as bloodthirsty as hell.

Without warning slugs cleaved the air. Bolan darted in among a stand of cypress trees, hauling Belle with him. A wide trunk offered cover. Once again he employed the scope and trained it on a break in the vegetation 120 feet away. The instant a loping form appeared, he fired. Whether he hit it or not, he couldn't say. And he didn't stick around to find out.

"Why are we running?" Belle demanded when he resumed their flight. "We should stay and finish it."

"It's four to one."

"So? Don't tell me you're scared?"

The thump of a heavy object striking the ground somewhere to their rear demonstrated the Scorpions were close enough to use grenades. Bolan dived, one arm around Belle. They had hardly struck the ground when the night resounded to a thunderous blast. Clods of dirt and bits of trees and brush rained down, pelting their heads and shoulders.

"Grenade," Bolan needlessly declared. He had an inkling of where it came from. Removing one of his own from his blacksuit, he hurled it stiff-armed in a high looping toss. Again the woods were buffeted by an explosion.

Belle no longer wanted to make a stand. She leaped up when he did and together they sprinted southward. They hadn't gone far when a swarm of leaden hornets tried to fatally sting them. On the fly, the Executioner reciprocated the favor.

Another hundred feet or so, and Bolan would make for the Jeep. A bend in the shoreline effectively hid them from the Scorpions, and he poured on the speed. He couldn't push himself to his limit because Belle wouldn't be able to keep up. But they were moving at a brisk clip when she suddenly tripped. Her fingers were torn from his grasp, and she involuntarily cried out.

Belle lay on her side, clutching her hurt shoulder and grimacing in torment. "I didn't see that rock."

"Keep moving," Bolan urged, boosting her up.

Belle was game, but she favored her left ankle and she couldn't run as fast as before. Bolan had to support her with his shoulder. They gained ten yards. Twenty yards. Then another grenade landed in the woods on their right, and Bolan did the only thing he could to save their lives. Whirling, he bounded to the water's edge and leaped head-first into the lake. Chilly water engulfed them, cushioning them from the terrible force of the blast. Shards peppered the surface, but the worst they suffered were some stinging bruises.

Bolan jammed his shoes against the bottom and surged upward. The water was only chest deep. Belle came up beside him, sputtering and gasping, and went to say something. In a blur, he clamped his left hand over her mouth and sank down again, dragging her with him.

Not all the way under, though. Their nostrils and eyes poked from the lake like those of twin bullfrogs.

A pair of camouflage-clad men trotted around the bend. One was tall and broad-shouldered, the other thin and winsome. Abreast of where Bolan and Belle were crouched, they halted. Moments later a short, a muscular form glided from the trees and joined them.

"Where the hell are they?" whispered the leader, the woman.

"I think my last grenade got them," the third Scorpion said.

"You don't see their bodies, do you, Rico? They must be up ahead." She scanned the woodland. "Where did Placer get to?"

"He's covering the road," the tall one whispered.

Kyle Carson, Bolan deduced. The short one had to be Rico Fuentes. Bolan couldn't rise up out of the lake quickly enough to drop all three before they retaliated. Not with his rifle under water and one hand bracing Belle.

"Why are we bothering with these two?" Fuentes asked. He was armed with an H&K MP-5. "We took care of Rabican. We've earned our money. Let's get out of here."

"I don't like leaving witnesses," the woman responded.

"What does it matter? They didn't get a good look at us." Fuentes gestured. "I vote we go."

"Since when did this become a democracy?"

Carson put a hand on her shoulder. "I agree with him, Maddy. We've wasted too much time as it is. Let's split while we can."

The distant wail of a siren accented his point. The woman swore, then rose and jogged into the trees. Fuentes and Carson looked at each other. The former Ranger shrugged, and they followed her.

Bolan slowly uncurled and hoisted Belle out of the lake. She placed her cheek on his shoulder and breathed deep, her fingers touching his neck. After half a minute he warily moved onto shore. They were both dripping wet.

Belle shivered and wrapped her arms around herself.

"So one of the Scorpions is a woman?" she whispered. "How very interesting."

The siren was growing louder and was being echoed by another sheriff's cruiser farther off.

Bolan gave them five minutes, if that. He helped up Belle and headed for the road, halting repeatedly to look and listen. She leaned on him most of the way. Her wound was taking it toll and sapping her vitality; she was too weak to stand for long on her own.

Flashing lights had appeared on the horizon. Hustling to the Jeep, he slid Belle into the passenger side, ran around and hopped in. His clothes squished as he sat down. Shoving the M-16 behind them, he started the engine and wheeled from the meadow.

They couldn't go south. The deputies might stop them. So Bolan drove north. As they passed the curved driveway, he glimpsed a middle-aged man crawling down the center, one leg a ravaged stump.

"Pierre!" Belle exclaimed, sliding weakly against her window. "He has been with us many years and is one of Henri's lieutenants."

"You can cut the act," Bolan said, accelerating.

"Pardon?"

"I heard the maid. Rabican didn't order you inside. He sent her to ask you to go back in." It had confirmed Bolan's growing suspicion. "You're his partner. That's why you were in charge last night. That's why he treats you with kid gloves."

Belle smirked and sagged back against her seat. "You think you know everything, but you don't."

A quarter of a mile ahead a pair of taillights swerved onto the roadway and bore north. Bolan had an idea who was in the vehicle, and he sped up so as not to lose them. "I know this much. Now that Rabican is gone, you're in charge. But most of your soldiers have been wiped out. Once I turn you over to the authorities, it will be the end of your smuggling empire."

"You give me too much credit," Belle said. "And you underestimate our resources. We have five times as many men as you saw tonight. Enough to bury Carbou and deal with the vermin he hired to dispose of us."

"You won't be in a position to bury anyone," Bolan noted. "I'll take care of the Scorpions myself." After the bloodbath he'd witnessed, they had risen to the top of his list. He would keep after them until he brought them to bay, no matter how long it took.

"You amuse me. In your way you are as arrogant as my Henri." Belle spoke in an exhausted whisper. "But that is always the problem with men. They behave like bulls, but they are calves at heart. A wise woman can always lead men around by their nose rings."

She wasn't making much sense, and Bolan chalked it up to the aftereffects of her ordeal. He fell quiet so she could rest. The first chance he had, he would get her to a hospital. But for now he couldn't lose those taillights. The Scorpions couldn't be allowed to get away.

Before setting out, Bolan had carefully studied a map of Point Coupee Parish. Ten miles north of the oxbow lake was a small town, Bettenberg. It had no airport, no train depot. Unless the Scorpions planned to leave the state by car, they were obliged to swing west and take a secondary road back to Baton Rouge. A long drive, but they would be there by three or four in the morning.

Bolan glanced at the side mirror. The flashing lights were almost to the estate. He saw something else, too, something that made him stiffen and grip the steering wheel in both hands.

A car was bearing down on them from behind, its headlights off. And leaning out the passenger window was one of the Scorpions, holding a leveled rifle.

At Hal Brognola's knock the door to the condo opened and Agent Farrow admitted him. Over in a corner Agent Jennings was rifling a bookcase by opening each book and flipping through the pages. "Find anything?" Brognola inquired. They had uncovered a lot already but crucial information was missing. Such as the identities of the last two Scorpions.

"Not yet, sir."

Farrow led him toward a doorway in the far wall. "It's this way, sir. Per your instructions, we haven't notified the police."

The bathroom was sparkling clean except for a puddle on the floor and the body in the tub. "So this is our mastermind," Brognola said. Tim Considine's features were sculpted in disbelief at his own demise. He looked so frail, so ordinary, so pathetic, it was difficult to conceive of him as the brains behind a highly efficient bevy of assassins.

"So it would appear," Farrow said. "Carson and Fuentes

both made a number of phone calls to this address. And the requisition forms and other documents we've uncovered are in Considine's handwriting." She avoided looking directly at the corpse.

"What we don't know is why he did it."

"Perhaps we never will," Brognola said. He left the bathroom. "It's a shame you couldn't bring him in for questioning."

"His death certainly appears to be accidental," Farrow commented.

"That what they want us to believe."

"But why kill him, sir, after all the trouble he went to on their behalf? Why turn on their creator, like Frankenstein on his namesake?"

"Your analogy might be more appropriate than you imagine," Brognola responded. "Maybe Considine didn't want them hiring out for money. Maybe he threatened to turn them in so they silenced him. Ever heard that old saying, don't play with matches unless you want to get burned?"

"My grandfather said that a lot."

Brognola grunted. "You just lost five brownie points." He moved to the bedroom. Across from the bed was a home workstation complete with a desk and a computer. The monitor was ablaze with a bizarre fire-red screen saver. Several ghostly white words floated in the center. *"Iudicare Villanus,"* he read aloud, frowning. "My Latin is a little rusty. Any idea what it means?"

"To judge villains," Farrow translated.

"You don't say." Brognola nodded at the computer. "You've checked the hard drive, I take it?"

"I gave it a once-over, yes, but nothing jumped out at me. Our tech boys can go in deeper than I can. We'll take the whole unit back with us."

Brognola walked into the living room and nearly bumped into Jennings, who grinned fiendishly and wagged a book the size of *War and Peace*. "Spit it out, son, before you bust a gut."

"Pay dirt, sir," Jennings said, handing him the heavy volume.

It was Edward Gibbon's *The Decline and Fall of the Roman Empire*. An abridged version, yet still thousands of pages long. Brognola hefted it, then opened the volume at random. A square hole was in the center. Considine had gone to all the trouble of cutting out the middle of the pages. And nestled in the secret hideaway were three computer disks. Each had been labeled. On the first had been scrawled Overview: Goals versus Practical Priorities. On the second was written Candidates: Evaluation Reports, Psych Profiles and Background Information. On the last was simply Targets.

"Our Mr. Considine was an extremely thorough man," Farrow remarked.

"More power to him." Brognola handed the disks to her. "We're going back to Justice. It's going to be a long night. I want a complete breakdown on these, ASAP."

"Do you want me to call the police now, sir?" Jennings inquired.

Brognola thought about the pathetic figure in the tub. He thought about the sensational headlines that would be splashed across every major newspaper in the land if the truth of Considine's death became public knowledge. The entire government could be blamed for the misguided deeds of a lone deluded soul. The United Nations would get involved and rail about violation of international law and the need to impose sanctions. Far-fetched? Not at all, given the harsh political realities of the world in which they lived.

"Sir?" Jennings prodded. "Whom do I contact about this?"

"No one."

The junior agents swapped glances. "No one, sir?" Farrow requested clarification. "You want us to keep this to ourselves?"

"Turn in your reports as required, and I'll handle the rest." Brognola knew the chairman of the National Intelligence Council. Together they could sweep the whole mess under the rug with no one the wiser.

"Whatever you say, sir," Farrow said dubiously.

"I'd rather spare the country the spectacle of a swarm of journalistic vultures in a feeding frenzy, if you don't mind," Brognola said. "Wouldn't you?"

"I wasn't questioning your judgment, sir," Farrow said. "My grandfather also used to say that some secrets are better *kept* secret."

"I'd like to meet this grandad of yours one day. He sounds like a gentleman after my own heart."

"Would that you could, sir. He's buried at Arlington."

"It's nice to see his brains run in the family," Brognola said to lessen the sting of being reminded of her grandfather's death, and she blushed from chin to hairline. Shoving his hands into the pockets of his overcoat, he strode for the door.

There was still the not-so-little matter of the death squad to be dealt with, Brognola thought. If anyone could take them down, it was Bolan. He hoped to heaven his friend was on top of the situation, for all their sakes.

IT HAD NEVER OCCURRED to the Executioner the Scorpions had arrived in two vehicles. Yet that was exactly what they did. And as if that weren't oversight enough, he had been so intent on shadowing the first vehicle, he hadn't bothered to see if he was being shadowed, in return. It was another lapse in a night of lapses. Once the mission was over, he intended to sit down, take stock and hone his mind to its customary razor's edge. Anything less was suicidal.

The sedan roared down on them like a participant in the Indy 500 and pulled alongside. The Scorpion leaning out the passenger window wasn't one Bolan recognized, so it had to be the man called Placer. He had what appeared to be a Galil rifle, and he drilled several rapid bursts into the Jeep.

Only Bolan's quick thinking saved him. He slammed the gas pedal to the floor and the Jeep leaped forward like a Thoroughbred out of the starting gate. The rounds that would have cored his door struck the rear of the vehicle, instead.

Belle looked up in alarm and blurted something in French.

Its engine growling, the sedan shot in pursuit. Now that they had spotted it, the driver switched on its headlights. Suddenly it veered, trying to ram them.

A sharp flick of Bolan's wrists sent the Jeep to the left. The car missed their rear bumper by a whisker, and almost instantly the driver tried again. Once more Bolan swerved. It threw Belle against the far door. Swiftly she donned her seat belt, then clung to the dash.

More rounds spanged off metal.

Either Placer or the driver would cripple the Jeep eventually unless Bolan came up with a way of discouraging them. He glanced in the rearview mirror, watching the sedan intently, and when the driver whipped in behind them and gave the sedan more gas, he spun the steering wheel to the right and braked.

The sedan flew past, giving Placer no time to fire.

Bolan sped up again, unlimbering the Beretta as he did. In seconds he was alongside the other vehicle. Placer had twisted and was yelling at the driver. Too late, he heard the Jeep, spun around and attempted to bring the Galil into play.

Bolan squeezed the trigger twice and had the satisfaction of seeing the Scorpion jerk to the impacts, then slump over the door. The driver turned, and Bolan saw the man clearly for the first time. It was Fuentes. The Executioner took hasty aim but Fuentes accelerated madly, burning rubber in a bid to escape his companion's fate. Within seconds the sedan was doing over ninety and climbing.

The Jeep couldn't keep up. Bolan tried, but the sedan's engine had a lot more horsepower and Fuentes drove insanely, taking the next curve at what had to be well over one hundred miles per hour. Miraculously the sedan didn't crash. Weaving wildly, it raced down the next section of road, rapidly increasing its lead, and by the time it came to the next bend, Bolan realized he had no chance of catching it, and slowed.

Belle let out a breath she had been holding. "I thought we were done for. Your reflexes are uncanny."

Bolan didn't comment. He was disappointed his chance to put an end to the Scorpions had fallen through. Fuentes would overtake the others, and they would make themselves scarce. Tracking them down would take a lot more time and effort.

From a plastic tray on the console Bolan claimed his cell phone. He put in a call to Brognola's office and was informed the big Fed was out. The agent who answered had no idea where Brognola had gone or when he would be back. Bolan tried the big Fed's personal number next. As he tapped in the last digit, he discovered his phone needed recharging. He raised the phone to his ear, heard several peculiar beeps and it went dead.

Bolan remembered having a talk with an Army colonel once about jinxed missions. The colonel held the view that some missions were jinxed from the get-go, with everything that could go wrong going wrong. The only thing to do in such situations, the colonel maintained, was cut losses and head back to base.

Bolan had never been the superstitious sort, but he had to admit he was having an uncommon string of setbacks. The whole business with the streetwalker, the fiasco at the mansion and now this. Nothing was going as planned. He was always being placed on the defensive, always having to react to enemy initiatives instead of initiating decisive action himself. His best bet now was to get to a telephone and contact Brognola so Belle could be taken into custody. Once he was on his own, he would go after the Scorpions in earnest. And it just might be the head Fed had new information to impart, information that could end the whole affair that much sooner.

Belle was curled against the door, her head resting on her good arm. She winced when the Jeep hit a bump, then touched the dark stain on her shoulder.

On the spur of the moment Bolan brought the vehicle to a stop at the side of the road. Shifting into Neutral, he took his foot off the clutch. "Let's have a look at you," he said.

"I can get by," she insisted.

"It's not debatable." Bolan flicked on the overhead light and fished the first-aid kit from his duffel bag. It included a small set of scissors, which he used to carefully cut her dress.

"Do you have any notion how much this evening dress cost?" Belle asked lightheartedly. "More than most people earn in a month."

"Or smuggle in a day?" Bolan rejoined. The blood had dried, and the sheer silk was stuck to her skin as if bonded. He pried at it, but it refused to peel off. "You might want to bite down on something. This will hurt."

Belle wasn't pleased by his previous comment. "I do

what I must to survive in a world that doesn't offer many opportunities for women to get ahead."

"Bull," Bolan said gruffly. "Is that how you justify polluting the minds and bodies of all those who get hooked on the drugs your pipeline funnels? Plenty of women succeed in life without doing it illegally." He went to pull on the fabric, but she swatted his hand away.

"Who are you to judge me? You don't know what my life has been like. The hard choices I've had to make."

"Law-abiding women make the same hard choices every day," Bolan said, "and most have too much personal dignity to step over the line."

Belle's temper flared and she cocked her left hand to slap him, but didn't. "So that's what you think of me? I have no dignity, no honor? I am beneath contempt?"

"Your words, not mine," Bolan said. "You're a formidable woman. It's a shame you didn't use your intelligence and beauty for the benefit of humankind instead of simply lining your pockets."

"I wasn't given any choice," Belle said defensively. "It was either lose the man I loved or turn my back on any shred of decency I had left and stand by him. I tried to persuade him to pick another path, but he has always been extremely stubborn. So I did what any wife would do."

Bolan couldn't hide his surprise.

"Ah. I see you do not know everything . That's right, Badass. Henri Rabican is my husband. When he asked me to be his wife, he also asked me to change my name. You see, he wasn't fond of some of the things I had done, the reputation I had. So the former Blanche Dalcour became Mrs. Belle Rabican."

"Why isn't there any record of your marriage?"

"We saw no need to apply for a license. Henri and I were

young and very much in love, and a license is just a piece of paper, after all. He and I shared our vows before a minister. As far as we were concerned, that was enough." Belle grew thoughtful. "Back then I had such high hopes. I had left my past in New Orleans, and Henri had an uncle in construction. I saw myself as a housewife, believe it or not, with a brood of children and a happy home life." She sighed longingly. "But it was not to be. Henri liked making money the easy way, and he took up with the wrong crowd. Before long he was smuggling drugs. One thing led to another, and now he is one of the two most powerful smugglers in the state." She said the last with a trace of pride. "Or he was, until the Scorpions killed him."

Bolan believed her tale. Her sincerity was beyond question. But he felt little sympathy for her plight. "You should have stopped Henri early on. Threatened to turn him in if he didn't go straight. If he loved you, he would have."

"You didn't know my Henri. Once he put his mind to something there was no changing it. And I couldn't abide the thought of losing him. Call me weak. Call me foolish. I loved him, and I make no apologies to anyone." Sorrow deepened the few lines in Belle's exquisitely lovely face. "Now he has reaped his just deserts, some would say. He is gone and I am the sole head of the organization we built up."

"If you're smart, you'll make a deal with the Feds. Not many people get a third chance to start over."

"I don't want a third chance," Belle said. "I want the bastards who killed my Henri."

Bolan eased his thumbnail under an edge of the silk and pressed his forefinger down, pinching it between them. "Brace yourself."

"I'm a big girl. I can handle it."

"Here it goes," Bolan said. A sharp wrench, and the silk

came loose. Belle flinched but didn't cry out. The slug had penetrated the soft flesh above her clavicle, gouging a furrow two inches long and a quarter of an inch deep across her right shoulder. She had lost some blood and would be stiff and sore for a few weeks, but that was all. "The Feds will get you to a hospital so this can be stitched up."

"I don't suppose there is any way I can talk you out of turning me over to them?"

"Need you ask?" Bolan applied antiseptic, unrolled some gauze and wrapped it around her shoulder. Several pieces of medical tape were enough to hold the bandage in place. "This will have to do for now."

"Merci," Belle said, smiling. "I am in your debt again."

Closing the kit, Bolan shoved it into his bag.

"Where to now?"

"A small town called Bettenberg." Bolan pulled away from the shoulder and brought the Jeep to the speed limit. He had driven for a minute or two when he realized Belle was studying him with keen interest. "What's on your mind?"

"That steely exterior of yours hides the heart of an idealist. You are not quite the badass I thought you were. You care about people, even people like me."

"Think so?"

"You saved my life, didn't you?" Belle retorted. "What I can't quite figure out is *what* you are? You do not act like a cop. You haven't identified yourself or flashed a badge, as a Fed would do. So you're not a federal officer, either."

Bolan let her speculate to her heart's content. It did no harm.

"You keep saying you are going to turn me over to the law. Which makes me wonder by what legal right do you hold me here against my will?"

"Nice try."

"I am serious. I know nothing about you. If you are a federal agent, I demand you identify yourself. It is my right as a private citizen." Belle waited for a response, and when none came, she slowly nodded. "So this is how it is. You stand on a pedestal and preach to me about decency and dignity but have secrets of your own."

"I work with the Feds on occasion," Bolan stated, which was as much as she had a right to know.

"In what capacity? Are you a duly constituted law officer? Or is what you do as illegal as what I do?"

Bolan saw where her interrogation was leading. "Ever heard of a pot calling a kettle black? I'm sanctioned by the government, which is more than can be said about you and your smuggling operation."

"Sanctioned to what end? To apprehend lawbreakers? What were you doing at our mansion, anyhow? Paying a social visit?"

"You ask too many questions."

"A woman's prerogative, yes?" Belle leaned back, yawned and crossed her arms in her lap. "We will talk more on this later. Right now I'm sleepy." She closed her eyes and was soon breathing heavily.

Adrift in introspection, Bolan drove on.

HAL BROGNOLA WAS PROUD of his crew at the Justice Department. They were bright and talented, the cream of the investigative crop. When he assigned a job, they tore into it like starved wolves into a bone.

The disks belonging to Considine were encrypted, but Brognola's computer techs were equal to the task. He could have handed the job to Aaron Kurtzman at Stony Man Farm, but his Justice techs were superb. Regular updates were relayed to his office every thirty minutes or so, and they made fascinating reading.

Tim Considine had missed his calling. Instead of being an analyst for the National Intelligence Council, he should have been a tactician for the CIA or some other government agency that fielded operatives to deal with real-world crises. The man had gone about organizing his death squad with a thoroughness Brognola admired.

Under the guise of routine background requests, Considine had compiled an amazing amount of personal data on a lengthy list of candidates. The only common denominator was that every prospect had fallen from grace in one way or another and needed to redeem themselves in the eyes of the U.S. government.

Once he'd narrowed the field, Considine conducted interviews. Those who passed were called back again and fed a line about going to work for a clandestine unit answerable directly to the President. Considine figured they would be so grateful to get their lives back on track, they would do his bidding with no questions raised.

But that was only the beginning. Like a spider weaving an intricate web, Considine had used his position with the NIC to acquire documents that enabled him to obtain equipment, to send his people to training sessions, and even to permit them to take military flights overseas. And he did it all so cleverly, so expertly, no one caught on.

As incredible as it sounded, Considine hadn't been motivated by personal gain or greed. He had set up the Scorpions out of a sense of patriotism. In Considine's warped slant on reality, he was doing the country he loved a favor by disposing of her enemies. His intentions had been noble enough. Unfortunately for him, he selected people who didn't share his sense of duty.

The concept of a death squad operating from American shores was profoundly unsettling. The very name carried connotations of evil and a government gone amok.

Brognola could remember when death squads were routine media fodder. Hardly a month went by that the press hadn't reported on a new one in Colombia or Argentina or Peru. He remembered thinking how horrible it was, civilians being gunned down on the streets, and how grateful that nothing like it ever happened in the U.S.

The big Fed loved and was devoted to his country. Considine held the same beliefs. Considine loved America, too, but he hadn't been content with serving his country within the bounds of the law. He had gone overboard, and set himself up as America's judge, jury and executioner. For his folly he paid the ultimate price.

The Scorpions were the problem now. They had to be put out of operation before their existence became common knowledge. A third had been identified. George Placer, a former DEA agent. A rotten apple with no desire to make good.

Brognola consulted his wristwatch. On his return from the condo he had received word Bolan called, using the alias they agreed on, Mike Blanski. That had been more than an hour ago. Strange that Bolan hadn't called back since.

There was a knock at the door. At Brognola's hail, Farrow entered. She moved as if she were treading on eggs and her expression was intensely troubled.

"I take it you're not here to relay good news."

"It's about Jennings, sir. Remember my telling you he went through the rest of Considine's library and didn't find any more disks?"

Mystified, Brognola said, "I told him to wrap up his search and head back. What's the problem?"

"Considine had a stereo in the living room, along with a rack of CDs. Jennings went through them before he left. He found an unmarked CD hidden in a two-CD set on big band music."

"And?" Brognola said, impatient for the news.

"He brought it back with him. It was encrypted, sir, just like the disks. We suspected it was a backup copy of the information they contained. Not five minutes ago the code was broken. It contains background intel on other candidates Considine interviewed for his death squad."

"That's hardly cause for concern."

"You don't understand, sir. These were candidates for his *other* death squad."

Brognola could almost feel the blood drain from his face. "He formed two squads?"

"Yes, sir. Mr. Considine wasn't as naive as we thought. He took steps to cover himself if things went wrong. He enlisted two more people, sir, for the express purpose of eliminating the Scorpions if they ever turned on him." Farrow paused. "The Scorpion Killers, he called them. And we have reason to believe they're in Louisiana right this moment."

11

His name was Lance Ryker, and until the fateful day of the accident he had counted himself among the toughest mother's sons on the planet. He had been a Navy SEAL.

Ryker liked the Navy, loved the SEALs. Loved how he was pushed to the limits of his endurance and beyond. Loved that feeling of being special, of being among the elite. He'd have stayed a SEAL forever, or until his joints started to creak from old age, whichever came first. Then came the hush-hush Thailand op where he took a round from a CIS 50 machine gun in the left knee. Goodbye knee. Goodbye SEALs.

Ryker was given a cushy desk job, but it wasn't to his liking. He had gone from an elite warrior to a pencil pusher, and it rankled. When his enlistment was up he got out of the Navy. It had reached the point he couldn't stand the uniform, couldn't stand being reminded of his glory days. He had gone to work as an insurance salesman, of all things, and because he had been a SEAL and SEALs never did anything half-assed, he was soon making a six-figure income and not doing half bad.

But Ryker missed the old days, missed them terribly. Many a night he would sit in his apartment going through his photo albums and a bottle of whiskey, and would tumble into bed feeling hopelessly sorry for his lot in life and wishing to hell the round from that damn machine gun had blown out his brains instead of blown out his knee. He yearned more than anything to be back in harness, to feel the familiar thrill, to know he was making a crucial difference in the good fight to keep the free world free.

Wonder of wonders, his prayers were answered.

Out of the blue appeared Tim Considine of the National Intelligence Council, an outfit Ryker had never heard of but which Considine assured him was one of the most influential agencies in all of government. And to his astonishment, Considine offered him a job.

Ryker had been honest with the guy. He had pointed out he had a bum leg, and that he couldn't outrun a petrified turtle if he tried. Considine didn't care. He said Ryker was right for the job anyway, that Uncle Sam needed him for a top-secret assignment. He was to become a killer of killers.

Ryker had always been an exceptional marksman. He excelled at the range and in combat. And although his knee was useless, his eyes and his fingers worked just fine, and he could still hit a target the size of a quarter at two hundred yards.

"What we need you to do," Considine informed him, "is to be on call in case you're needed. I've explained about the Scorpions. How they're being given a second chance to prove themselves. Some might not make the grade. They might turn on their handler. Me. In which case they are to be terminated with extreme prejudice."

"How will I know if they've gone bad?" Ryker had asked.

"We'll set up a special E-mail account. Check it once a day, without fail. You should receive a blank E-mail from an address I'll supply, a sign all is well. If you don't receive a blank E-mail, you're to call a phone number I'll give you as a fail-safe. You will hear a recording instructing you how to proceed in hunting down the Scorpions and disposing of them."

"But didn't you say there are four Scorpions? What if only one or two go astray?"

"They were created to function as a unit. As a unit they will live and die," Considine said philosophically. "Now, are you game? Will you help your country if the need should arise?"

What else could Ryker say? He gladly accepted and was teamed with a former SWAT officer from the Windy City who had been discharged when he accidentally shot a civilian during a hostage situation at a bank. Sam Winslow was his name, and the higher-ups at the Chicago PD had accused him of being too reckless and not following procedure.

Ryker and Winslow. The Scorpion Killers, Considine called them.

Now there they were in the Louisiana backcountry in a rented car, out to kill a squad of professional assassins. A job made ridiculously easy by Considine.

The daily E-mail had failed to arrive, and Ryker had phoned the special number. He reached a recording, made by Considine. It supplied the home addresses of all four Scorpions. "They're involved in an illicit enterprise in Louisiana," Considine had revealed. "I know more than they think I do. Including where Maddy Culver has been staying in Baton Rouge."

Trailing Culver and Carson from the motel had been child's play. Ryker had witnessed the attack on the mansion from a discreet distance, and when it was over, he had followed the Scorpions northward. He had seen a Jeep pull out far ahead of him, had seen the running gunfight between the driver of the Jeep and the Scorpions in the second vehicle. Not knowing what to make of it, he had dropped back. He had pulled over when the Jeep did, and gone on when the Jeep went on.

Now Winslow turned and remarked, "You've let the Scorpions get too far ahead." His black skin was nearly invisible in the darkened car. "We'll lose them."

"So what if we do?" Ryker responded. "We know who they are. We know where they live. If we don't finish the job here, we'll stake out their homes one by one." The important thing was not to rush. Considine had stressed they had to take it nice and slow. Given they were up against seasoned assassins, any lapse could be their last. "There's no time element involved. We'll get them sooner or later."

"What about the big fella in the Jeep? Do you figure he must be one of the smuggler's gunnies?"

"No," Ryker answered. From their vantage point in a clearing in the woods they had seen the big guy arrive, hide the Jeep in the meadow and slink off toward the lake. After the mansion blew, a firefight had broken out, and the same guy and a woman emerged, jumped into the Jeep and off they went. "Call me nuts, but I think he's after the Scorpions, same as us."

"How can that be? Think maybe he's working for Considine, the same as us?"

"Considine would have told us," Ryker said. But then again, maybe not. Considine was a man of many secrets. It was entirely possible they weren't the only fail-safe.

"What do we do? Eliminate him, too?"

"I suggest we play it by ear. Keep after the Scorpions and wait to see what develops. Who knows? Maybe this big guy will do our job for us."

"I suppose that's best," Winslow said. He was large in his own right and had the shoulders of a linebacker. "If this fella gets in our way, though, I say we take him down and sort it all out later."

"My thinking exactly."

THE EXECUTIONER WAS three miles out of Bettenberg when he came over a hill doing seventy and was stunned to see someone lying across the road ten car-lengths ahead. Automatically he tromped on the brakes. The Jeep slid sideways, its tires screeching, and the reek of burning rubber filled the inside.

Bolan spun the wheel to compensate, and the vehicle went into a spin. He fought it without success and was slammed against the bucket seat. Trees danced in the headlights. Then the Jeep straightened out. He regained control in time to miss the body by a whisker. He saw camouflage fatigues and combat boots and a web belt. It was Placer, the Scorpion he had shot, dumped there to slow him.

The Scorpions had set a trap.

Suddenly the windshield burst into hundreds of shards. Rounds ripped into the dash, into the door, into the roof. Bolan heard Belle yell, but whatever she said was lost amid the racket. Both rear tires were blown out from under them.

Again the Jeep slid. The trees loomed nearer. Bolan tried to steer into an opening, but it wasn't wide enough. "Hold on!" he shouted.

The collision crumpled both fenders and threw the soldier against the steering wheel. Pain speared his ribs. More rounds struck the rear of the Jeep. Shadowy shapes were bounding across the road toward them.

Belle was dazed. Both hands on the dash, she shook her head to clear it.

Lunging past her, Bolan worked the knob to her door and flung it wide. He tore at her seat belt, grabbed her by the shoulder and shoved. As he started to reach for the M-16, he saw one of the Scorpions halt, hold an object close to his chest and jerk at it.

Bolan exploded from the Jeep. He forgot about the M-16, forgot about his duffel bag, forgot everything except the urgent need to cover as much ground as humanly possible in the shortest amount of time. Belle had fallen onto her side and was standing. Without breaking stride he caught hold of her and raced into the woods. He didn't care where he ran, he just ran, crashing through brush that barred his path. In his mind's eye he ticked off the yards. Five. Ten. Twenty. Suddenly a short slope fell before him and without slowing he sprang to the lip and out into space. Belle shifted as he leaped, and they came down off balance. He tried to cushion her as best he was able but lost his hold as they tumbled.

Simultaneously the grenade went off. It had to have ignited the Jeep's gas tank because there was a second, louder blast, and sheets of flame roiled heavenward.

Bolan rolled to a stop against a tree. Ignoring a sharp pain in his hip, he was on his feet and had turned toward Belle before the booming echoes died. Grabbing her waist, they ran. He had lost the rifle and the night-vision scope, as well as the contents of his bag, but he still had the Beretta and the Desert Eagle and a couple of grenades. It put him at a distinct disadvantage, though. The Scorpions had superior firepower and greater range in their favor.

The Executioner covered another twenty-five yards, then paused. There was a chance the Scorpions hadn't seen them flee and believed they were dead. He strained his ears for the sound of a car and instead heard the rustle of vegetation from several different directions. Carson, Fuentes and Culver were coming after them.

A glance at the stars told Bolan he had been bearing almost due east. He angled northeast, intending to eventually loop back to the road. Belle clung to him with both arms, her breath warm on his neck. The feel of her body had no effect, as it had previously, which was how it should be.

"You saved my life again," she whispered.

"Be quiet," Bolan said, but she didn't obey.

"Why did they ambush us?"

The answer was self-evident. Fuentes had caught up to Carson and Culver, and the three of them elected to end it then and there. Or else the woman had. She was the leader, and she had already demonstrated she had a lust for blood. Bolan didn't tell Belle as much. He moved on, picking his route with care, making as little noise as his skill allowed.

All went well for a while. The forest had gone quiet, and Bolan was half convinced he had given the Scorpions the slip when he rounded a thicket and a four-legged form snorted and bolted to the north, crashing headlong through the undergrowth. He glimpsed antlers a split second before the buck disappeared.

Almost instantly an SMG chattered and slugs buzzed to their left.

Bolan flattened, yanking Belle down with him. Rolling onto his back, he drew the Beretta and held it in a two-handed grip. The forest was still again. Even the insects had gone quiet. He probed the shadows, seeking telltale movement. He was rewarded with a flicker, and a partial silhouette sprouted from the trunk of an oak forty feet away. Extending the Beretta, he centered the sound suppressor and curled his finger to the trigger.

Suddenly, much nearer, a twig crunched. Out of the corner of his right eye Bolan spied another darkling shape, this one almost parallel with their position and so close the Scorpion was bound to hear the Beretta if he fired at the first figure. He started to swivel to take out the closest threat when he spotted the third Scorpion a dozen yards to their left.

Belle gripped his wrist.

The Executioner held his fire. The Scorpions were moving past their position. The one on the right, so slender it had to be Culver, pumped her arm in a signal and the other two melted into the vegetation. So did she a heartbeat later. They made no noise. Freezing in position Bolan let a suitable interval go by. Then he slowly rose into a crouch and scanned the area. The Scorpions appeared to be gone. He plucked at Belle's arm and she rose.

The wind had picked up. Nearby trees swayed and rustled. Bolan took his bearings by the North Star and crept toward the road. They were almost there when an engine cranked over north of them. Hastening on, he saw a pair of taillights receding toward Bettenberg.

"Did they give up?" Belle whispered.

"So it seems." Wary of a trick, Bolan didn't move into the open just yet.

"At least you got one of the bastards." Belle was staring toward the spot where Placer's body had been. The other Scorpions had taken it with them. "One down, only three to go."

Much to Bolan surprise, another engine turned over, this

time to the south. He ducked behind a bush, and Belle had the good sense to follow his example. In a few seconds a car drove past, traveling north. Its headlights were off, and so were the dash lights. Bolan saw a pair of dim outlines, nothing more. Someone else was stalking the Scorpions.

"Who in the world are they?" Belle wondered.

"Some of your people from the mansion?"

"The few who were still left were in no shape to drive," Belle noted. "No, it must be someone we don't know about. Maybe Carbou sent a couple of his boys to keep tabs on them."

As if Bolan didn't have enough to contend with. The sound of the engine faded, and he stepped onto the road and walked to where the Jeep had crashed. Little was left. Part of the frame, an axle, and two smoldering tires.

"I guess we walk to Bettenberg, eh?" Belle said and trudged off. Her evening dress was a ruin. The torn fabric at her shoulder flapped as she walked, and the entire dress was smeared with dirt and grass stains.

"Maybe not," Bolan said. Moving past her, he scoured the woodland on both sides. A dull glint of glass and metal helped him locate the car Fuentes had driven, a late-model coupe. It had been driven in among the trees and abandoned. The doors were unlocked. He slid in and frowned. The keys weren't there.

"I'll flip you to see who jump-starts it," Belle said.

Bolan handled the chore himself. Backing out, he drove north, his headlights on. The Scorpions and the occupants of the mystery vehicle were too far ahead to spot them by now.

"I must say," Belle dryly commented, "being your prisoner isn't boring. But I can't help thinking that I'm more bother than I'm worth. You've been holding back, haven't you? Not engaging them for fear of harm befalling me?"

"So?"

"So you would be smart to let me out so we can go our separate ways," Belle advised. "I hold no grudge against you. It is the Scorpions I want, and the Scorpions I will have."

"The Feds will have a say in that," Bolan said.

"Only if you turn me over to them, right? It's not too late to come to your senses. No one need ever know."

"I would."

"A man of principle. I wish my Henri had been more like you. But he wasn't, and I have to live with that. Just as you must live with the knowledge I won't permit you to place me in the custody of the authorities."

"Fair enough," Bolan said. She was welcome to object all she wanted. In another couple of miles he would place a call to Brognola, and that would be the end.

"Funny, isn't it, the decisions life forces us to make?" Belle said, more to herself than to him. "When we are young, we brim with ideals and long to make this world a better place in which to live. But the world doesn't want to change. It destroys ideals and wears down innocence until there is nothing left but cynicism."

Bolan looked at her profile highlighted against the window. "Speak for yourself. The world can't beat us down if we don't let it."

"You wouldn't say that if you had seen some of the things I have."

"Really? Have you ever seen what was left of a ten-year old girl who stepped on a land mine in a combat zone? Or gone through a village after rebels finished torturing every man, woman and child? Ever seen people lined up in front of a firing squad and executed? Or been to the detox ward of a hospital, where many of the addicts who use the drugs you smuggle end up?"

Belle pursed her lips in resentment. "It always comes back to that, doesn't it? To the smuggling?"

"To the lives you've destroyed, yes. To the families who go without food and clothes in order for the parents to support their habit. To the women who sell themselves on the street for enough for their next fix. To all those who overdose," Bolan stated. "I could go on and on, but why bother."

"Why, indeed?" Belle said spitefully. "I misjudged you. I took you for someone who understood the ways of this world. But you're one of those holier-than-thou types who looks down on everyone who doesn't meet their high standards."

Bolan knew the ways of the world, as she called them, all too well. But arguing would be pointless. She couldn't seem to get it through her head there were lines that shouldn't be crossed no matter what. Belle was one of those who saw everything in shades of gray. She could justify any deed, no matter how criminal, by claiming she wasn't left any choice. Yes, she was a drug smuggler, but only because her husband made her do it. She loved Rabican so much, she just had to go along with whatever he did. Her love was a convenient scapegoat for all manner of evil.

Sadly there were millions more exactly like her, Bolan knew. Well-meaning but deluded, they had lost the ability to tell the difference between right and wrong. Every motive was relative, so every act was condoned. Small wonder crime was epidemic and growing worse by the decade. Small wonder politicians who lied and stole and misrepresented their constituents were reelected over and over. Small wonder the basic rights Americans once held so dear were no longer deemed relevant.

A sign appeared. Bettenberg lay a mile off. Soon they

were driving by quaint homes with neatly kept yards, and the speed limit dropped from fifty-five to thirty-five. They reached the town limits. Bettenberg's population was posted as 812, and the downtown district, such as it was, mirrored that fact. Two dozen small stores, a couple of markets and a bank lined the single main street. At that hour of the night the sidewalks had been rolled up, and most of Bettenberg's populace was sound asleep. The fire station was dark, the police station had a lone light on.

Bolan saw no sign of the Scorpions or the car that had been following them. He did spot a phone booth a block to the west and wasted no time pulling in next to it. "I want you to come with me," he commanded.

"Afraid I'll drive off on you?" Belle laughed and winked. "I would, too."

Bolan waited until she slid out, then did likewise. The folding door to the phone booth was closed. When he opened it, an small overhead bulb came on. He dipped his hand into a hidden pocket for the calling card he had been given under the name of Blanski, and lifted the receiver.

"Uh-oh. It looks as if the local constabulary finds us interesting."

At the next intersection a black-and-white had braked, and a young policeman was giving them the once-over.

"Let's show him how friendly we are," Belle said and cheerfully waved.

The patrol car wheeled toward them.

Bolan stepped out of the booth and swung the door midway shut so the light went out. He was still armed with the Desert Eagle and the Beretta, to say nothing of the grenades clipped to his belt, and he'd rather the officer didn't see them. He could ill afford to spend a night in jail, or however long it took for Brognola to get him out.

Belle had taken a couple of steps and was beaming like the policeman was her long-lost cousin.

"I'm warning you," Bolan said.

"I'm being friendly, is all." Belle took another step. "I don't want him prying into our affairs any more than you do."

The black-and-white's tires crunched to the curb, and the patrolman climbed out. He was fresh out of the academy, if Bolan was any judge, with crew cut sandy hair and a nightstick he swung at the end of a lanyard. "Howdy, folks," he greeted them. "We don't see many up and about at this hour."

"We're just passing through," Bolan informed him.

"I gathered as much." The young policeman looked Bolan up and down. "Is that body armor you've got on, sir?" he politely inquired, his right hand straying to his hip an inch above the butt of a .44 Magnum Smith & Wesson stainless-steel Model 629 revolver.

Before Bolan could answer, Belle moved to the officer's side, saying, "Oh, he's got a lot more than that. You should ask about his guns."

"Guns?" the patrolman repeated.

Bolan guessed what she was up to, but he couldn't make any quick moves to stop her or the cop might go for his gun. "I can explain—" he began.

"Don't forget to ask about his grenades," Belle added, taking a half-step behind the alarmed patrolman. "They make an awfully loud noise when they go off."

The young cop stiffened. "You have hand grenades, sir? I'm afraid I'll have to ask you to put your hands on your head and turn around."

To do otherwise invited trouble. Bolan slowly lifted his arms, palms out to show he was friendly. He would no more harm an honest cop than he would beat a baby. "I work for the government. There's a number you can call at the Justice Department to confirm it."

"First things first. We'll sort this out at the station after I disarm you."

"Do your duty," Belly urged, slipping behind him. "But while we're on the subject of disarming, what's a boy like you doing with a cannon like this?" At that, she snaked the Smith & Wesson from its holster as slick as a pickpocket and jammed the muzzle against the cop's neck.

"What are you doing, lady?" the bewildered patrolman asked.

"What you think I be doing, boy?" Belle rejoined, resorting to a Cajun dialect. "Joli, there, is the noble sort. But he won't lift a finger against me so long as I can blow your head clean off."

"What is this all about?" The young cop was trying to be brave but not entirely succeeding. "Give back my weapon before you find yourself behind bars."

"I wouldn't do anything hasty, if I was you," Belle cautioned. "Not unless you can dodge a bullet at point-blank range." She thumbed back the hammer to convince him she was serious, then backpedaled toward his patrol car, pulling him after her.

Bolan started toward them but stopped when Belle pointed the revolver at him.

"Ah, ah, ah," she scolded. "This is where we part ways." She sighted down the barrel, then smiled. "The only reason I don't end your life right this moment is I owe you. You saved my hide. I spare yours. More than fair?"

"You'll never get away, lady," the young cop said. "We'll put out an APB and have you in custody before morning."

"God loves an optimist," Belle declared. She stopped and wriggled her fingers under the policeman's nose. "Fork over your keys. And be quick about it. I have places to go, people to kill."

"I can't do that."

"You will do it, or you'll die." Belle touched the muzzle to his head. "Is that a wedding ring on your finger? Do you really want to leave your wife a widow? Your children fatherless?"

Bolan didn't blame the younger man for caving in. They stood and watched as Belle started up the cruiser, pulled up next to the coupe and calmly shot out the near-side front tire so he couldn't give chase.

"It's been fun, Badass!" Belle whooped and departed in a spray of dust, her blond hair flying.

The young policeman's mouth was agape. "That's some woman, mister!"

"You don't know the half of it," Bolan said.

Madeline Culver was ready to scream. Everything had been going so well. They had flawlessly executed a coordinated assault on the Rabican estate. With her own eyes she had seen Henri Rabican at a second-floor window when the C-4 went off and witnessed the roof and walls crash down on top of him. They had fulfilled their contract. They had earned their pay.

But she hadn't been content with that.

Culver knew the blonde in the fancy dress was Rabican's paramour, thanks to intel provided by Considine. Culver had the floozy dead to rights, had wounded her, in fact, and would have finished her off if not for the big man who came out of nowhere to spirit the bimbo toward the lake, and safety.

Never one to leave a job half finished, Culver insisted on going after them. Fuentes and Placer bitched, but they did as she wanted. She thought it would be a quick clean-and-sweep. Instead, the pair gave them the slip. It didn't sit well with her.

She hated failure. It was why she had cheated on her crucial exam at the police academy. Even though she knew the material as well as could be expected, she was so afraid of flunking out, she took the drastic step of writing snippets of information on her forearms. Twice she hiked her sweater sleeve a few inches to verify an answer, and wasn't caught. The third time, the teacher happened to be standing right behind her. She had been so absorbed in the test, she hadn't noticed.

After being booted out of the academy, Culver drifted from job to job. Nothing interested her. Sales work bored her to tears. Secretarial work was beneath her. She craved an exciting job, a position that would keep her on the go and on her toes. That was why she wanted to be a cop in the first place.

The day Considine showed up at her door was her fondest desire come true. She heard him out, and although she wondered how it was the government would even consider hiring a group of rejects and misfits for a special strike force, she agreed to join if for no other reason than to alleviate her boredom.

Right away, Culver deduced there was more to the Scorpions than Considine let on. He had been a strange one. A geek who thought he was Richard the Lionheart. A crusader on a personal campaign to stamp out evil. She questioned him now and again, tactfully of course, and bit by bit learned enough to confirm her suspicions.

About the time she realized the Scorpions were a sham was about the same time she decided to take the bone fate had thrown to her and run with it. She had been given an opportunity to make more money than she ever dreamed of, and she would be an idiot to let it pass her by. Convincing Fuentes and Placer had been easy enough. They were as mercenary at heart as she was. Kyle had taken longer, even though he loved her. The thick vein of morality that ran through his core had to be chipped away piece by piece until he gave in.

Culver regretted having to kill Considine. Not a lot. Unwittingly he had taught her a great deal. Enough for her to set the wheels in motion to make them all rich, and to have him disposed of when he dared object.

It had taken months to line up their first client. Many prospective employers were naturally hesitant about hiring a death squad that had spent a year assassinating their own kind. Lafe Carbou wasn't one of them. He had been desperate. Rabican was outwitting him at every turn, and eventually Rabican would become the undisputed kingpin of Gulf Coast smugglers unless Carbou took action.

Enter the Scorpions.

Culver worked out the deal. Half the money up front, the other half when the job was done. They were to phone Carbou and give him final payment instructions once Rabican was disposed of. Culver figured on having it in her hands by midnight. She hadn't figured on losing one of her team.

The big guy who had saved the blonde was to blame. Fuentes had caught up to Culver and honked his horn until she pulled over. Placer's death was a shock. Fuentes said the big guy was still after them in a Jeep, so Culver came up with the idea of laying an ambush. The guy wouldn't be expecting it. He'd be easy to take down.

The woman had seldom been so wrong about anyone. The big guy was anything but easy. He had whisked the blonde out of the Jeep and into the woods before Fuentes could lob a grenade. Then he had eluded their best efforts to hunt him down, outwitting them at their own game. Aware they had wasted too much time, Culver had called off the hunt. But God, she hated failure.

She decided to contact Carbou, settle accounts and get the hell out of Louisiana. But when she punched in the number on her cell phone, the goon who answered gave her the runaround. He claimed Carbou wasn't available and suggested she call back. Then he had the gall to hang up.

Culver quelled an impulse to scream and shook the phone as if she were strangling it.

"What's the matter?" Carson asked.

They were at a gas station half a mile beyond Bettenberg. Taking turns in the run-down establishment's only rest room, they had shed their combat gear and donned civvies. No sense in attracting undue attention.

Fuentes was leaning against the fender. "What did Carbou say? When do we get our bread?"

"What we have here," Culver said, quoting from an old movie while punching in the number again, "is a failure to communicate."

The same bozo answered. She gave it to him straight. "Listen up, you son of a bitch. Either put your boss on right this second or his smuggling days are over. You get me?"

The goon covered the phone, but his voice was clear enough for Culver to hear him say, "It's her again, boss. What do I tell her?"

The line seemed to go dead, and she thought they had added slight to insult by hanging up on her again. Then Carbou's raspy voice came on, and she sensed by his tone things had gone sour.

"What you want, missy? Why you be bothering Carbou?"

"Save the Cajun jargon for your Neanderthals," Culver spit. "You know damn well what I want. Tell us how we can pick up the rest of our money." The first half had been delivered to a remote drop in New Orleans by a carload of Carbou's errand boys more than a week ago.

"Rabican is dead?"

"Would I be calling if he wasn't?" Culver was so angry, she could hardly think straight. "So let's hear it."

"There's been a slight change in plans, missy," Carbou said in his condescending fashion. "The amount we agreed on is too much."

Culver's blood boiled in her veins. She couldn't believe what she was hearing.

"You agreed to our terms," she reminded him. "You paid half up front."

"And now that I have thought about it some more, half is what the job was worth. Be content with the two hundred thousand. It's all you are going to get."

"You're a dead man, Carbou," Culver flatly told him.

"What will you and your friends do, missy? Try to kill me? Do so, and your secret will be made known to the whole wide world."

"What are you blowing smoke about?"

"You and your Scorpions, missy. I bet the newspapers would be very interested in hearing how you kill for money. Come anywhere near me, and I will have word leaked to the press."

"You're bluffing. The police would get involved, and an investigation would implicate you in Rabican's death."

"Who will tell them? You and your friends? You are the ones who did the actual killing. It will go worse for you than for me." Carbou chuckled. "I am not as dumb as you think, woman. The only two at my end who know I hired you are trusted lieutenants. So you see, as the saying goes, I have you over a barrel. And I save myself two hundred thousand dollars." Laughing, he hung up.

Culver almost threw the phone to the ground. They had been played for suckers, and unless they did something about it, no one would ever take them seriously again.

"What's up, hon?" Carson looked worried.

"We're going to New Orleans," Culver announced.

"To collect the money?" Fuentes asked.

"To kill a scumbag."

THERE HAD BEEN A TIME when Mack Bolan was entirely on his own. A lone wolf with a personal mission, he had waged a one-man war on the insidious influences trying to undermine America and all she stood for.

Then the government intruded itself. Bolan began working with Brognola on a steady basis. And while he occasionally missed the old days and the freedom from accountability that came with it, he had to admit there were instances when cooperating with the Feds had its advantages. An hour and twenty minutes after Belle Rabican stole the police car, Bolan was back in the coupe and on the move.

The three-man Bettenberg police force hadn't taken kindly to having one of their patrol cars stolen. Nor were they very happy that Bolan was running around the Louisiana countryside with enough weapons and explosives to wipe out half their town. But a phone call to Washington allayed their fears, and under the mistaken belief Bolan was a full-fledged agent with the Justice Department, they roused the owner of the local tire store out of bed and had him put a new tire on the coupe.

While they were waiting, Bolan offhandedly mentioned he needed to charge his cell phone. The next thing he knew, he was being whisked to the local electronics shop. The proprietor showed up in a robe and slippers and eagerly offered to supply a new charger.

Bolan begged off, noting it would take a couple of hours

to charge the battery and he didn't have that much time. So the man gave him a new, fully charged battery instead.

Bolan felt guilty about misleading them, but he hadn't done it deliberately. The cops had leaped to the conclusion he was a Fed on an important case, and took it from there. He thanked them as he climbed into the coupe, and the police chief, a kindly, gray-haired fellow with a perpetual smile, clapped him on the back and said, "Think nothing of it. We're glad to be of help. We might be a bunch of small-town hicks, but we know what matters and we do our part for Uncle Sam."

Bolan thought about their kindness as he drove off. The chief was much too modest. Their willingness to help, to go out of their way for him, was a living example of America at her best. Decent, upright people, doing what had to be done with no thought of personal gain.

Whenever the wear and tear of the War Everlasting got to him, whenever he was tempted to wonder why he bothered, Bolan would think of people just like them, of the families struggling to make ends meet, the single moms juggling jobs and parenthood, the innocents everywhere who never harmed another soul and only wanted to be left in peace to live their lives as they saw fit. They were the people he was fighting to protect. They were the reason he put his life in jeopardy time and again. For their sakes no sacrifice was too great or too small.

On leaving Bettenberg Bolan headed south. Brognola had asked him to call as soon as he could talk freely, so he put the new battery to the test and tapped in the big Fed's number. "It's me," he said when the head Fed answered.

"You're lucky those cops were so understanding and I didn't have to bail your butt out of the slammer," Brognola remarked. "Are you on the road again?"

"New Orleans or bust."

"Good. We've uncovered a lot at this end. It's a whole new ball game. New players have entered the picture, and you'd best stay out of their crosshairs."

"Break it down," Bolan said.

Ten minutes later the soldier hung up and pondered what he had learned. The occupants of the mystery car tailing the Scorpions were no longer a mystery. It had to have been the Scorpion Killers, Ryker and Winslow.

Brognola believed the Scorpions were on their way home, and he had agents waiting for each of them at their apartments. Agents were also waiting for Ryker and Winslow. The Scorpion Killers might get to the Scorpions first, but there was nothing anyone could do about that. One way or another, in a few hours the entire business would be wrapped up.

That left Lafe Carbou.

Bolan was on his way to New Orleans. An informant had supplied the Feds with a list of Carbou's haunts, and Brognola had relayed the intel. Ordinarily, disposing of a rabid wolf like Carbou involved a simple stalk and kill. But this time there was a complication in the vengeful form of Belle Rabican.

The soldier knew Belle wouldn't rest until she killed the man responsible for her husband's death. She would launch an all-out war if she had to. And if civilians happened to get caught up in it, that was their tough luck.

A yawn nipped at Bolan's mouth, and he shook his head to dispel tendrils of fatigue. He intended to drive straight through to New Orleans, get a motel room and sleep until evening. Then the hunt would begin.

Lowering the window, Bolan breathed deep of the crisp night air. He switched on the radio and fiddled with the tuner until he found a station to his liking. A song by the Rolling Stones came on and he hummed along, tapping his fingers on the steering wheel in time to the music.

Unexpectedly Bolan's cell phone beeped. Thinking it was Brognola, Bolan answered quickly.

"Do you miss me? I thought you were real glad to get rid of me, the way you whisked me onto that bus and all."

For one of the few times in recent memory, Bolan was dumbfounded.

"Are you still there, mister? I wish you'd told me your name. Giving me this number to call in an emergency was great but I like to know who I'm talking to."

"Nina?"

"In the flesh. Well, okay, not really in the flesh since we're talking on the phone."

"Where are you?" Bolan broke in. He had bought her bus ticket to Chicago and given her three hundred dollars to tide her over. He never thought he would hear from her again.

"Back home. At my place."

"In Baton Rouge? What about your aunt in the Windy City?"

"She must have moved." Nina laughed as if it were hugely funny. "A little voice in the back of my head kept telling me to call her before I took off to make sure it was okay to visit, but I never did. It's been years since I last talked to her. I'm sort of the black sheep of my family, and no one wants anything to do with me."

"Nina," Bolan said, but she didn't seem to hear.

"Anyway, this really nice guy on the bus let me use his phone and I called, but guess what? I got a recording saying my aunt's phone number had been disconnected. I guess she moved and never told me where she was going."

"Nina?"

"I thought about calling my sister in L.A., but she and I don't hit it off too well. She blames me for the time her hubby came on to me, although I swear to God I wasn't hitting on him or anything. He's just your basic lech—"

"Nina!" Bolan snapped to get her attention. "Why didn't you rent a room somewhere? Baton Rouge isn't safe for you."

"I know, I know. But it's where I live. I have friends here. And, well, I sort of used most of the money you gave me to buy a new pair of shoes. You should see them. They're the sweetest set of pumps. Absolutely to die for."

"Is that why you called? To tell me about your new shoes?"

"Oh, no." Nina giggled hysterically. "How silly do you think I am? You said I was only to call this number if I was in trouble, and I think I am. There are some guys in a car across the street, watching my place."

"Some of Rabican's men?" Bolan wondered aloud.

"I don't know. I didn't ask them." Fear crept into her voice. "I snuck in the back way and didn't turn on any lights so they must not know I'm here. I'm still a little scared, though. What do I do?"

Bolan happened to pass a mile marker and did some quick computations. "Sit tight until I get there. I'm about an hour away."

Her relief was touching. "Thanks, mister. I'm sorry to have bothered you. It's just that there's no one else who would give a damn."

"Mike," Bolan said.

"Sorry?"

"You can call me Mike."

BELLE RABICAN vowed Louisiana would run red with blood before she was done! She couldn't stop thinking of her husband as she raced toward Baton Rouge in the stolen police car. She couldn't stop reliving their many years together, the good times and the bad.

Most women would say Rabican wasn't much of a catch but Belle had loved him, heart and soul. He had a stubborn streak and a vicious temper, but he never once lifted a hand against her or treated her with anything other than respect and tenderness. As a lover, he was magnificent.

Rabican could snuff out a human life without batting an eye, and some people would say that was wrong. But not Belle. It was a dog-eat-dog world, and her husband had been at the top of the food chain. Together, they had carved out their own little empire. They made millions and lived like a king and queen. Their life had been wonderful until Carbou came along.

Carbou. The very name filled Belle with hatred such as she had never known. He was a pig, an upstart with delusions of grandeur. He wanted control of the whole state, and he would stop at nothing to acquire it.

Belle should have put out a contract on the bastard long ago. She had mentioned it to Rabican but he refused to hire outsiders. He took pride in handling problems himself. So he sent his own men, but Carbou was too crafty for them. In retrospect, Belle should have hired someone anyway. Her husband would still be alive.

Flashing lights ended Belle's trip down memory lane. She was near her estate. Every sheriff's car in the parish and a lot of other official vehicles, including two fire engines and three ambulances, were parked along the driveway or in front of what was left of the mansion, which was precious little.

Despite the risk, Belle slowed to a crawl. Most of the deputies and all the firemen were going through the debris. Victims on stretchers were being placed into two of the ambulances. As she looked on, the rotating lights on top of the third ambulance flared bright, and the siren let out a shriek. It roared toward the road, bound for the nearest hospital.

Belle pulled over to let it go by and turned the dash lights low. The ambulance driver smiled and waved. She waved back, wondering who was in the back and how bad off they were.

Charred and mangled bodies were being placed in rows between the rubble and the stable, then covered with plastic. Belle counted twenty-two. She thought of Claudette, her maid, and clenched her fingers so tight around the steering wheel that her knuckles grew pale.

About to drive on, Belle saw a deputy jogging toward her, waving. She quickly sped up, then watched in the side mirror. He stopped and scratched his head, plainly puzzled. Wheeling, he hurried to a cruiser, jumped in and came after her. She was concerned the deputy had heard the APB that young cop said he was going to send out. But if that were the case, why didn't other deputies rush to pursue her, too?

Belle went faster. She had to get over the hill to the south and out of sight of the mansion before she stopped. And she *had* to stop. If she didn't, the deputy would become even more suspicious and get on the horn to his fellow officers. She glanced at the police radio, which was off, and turned it on. Static crackled from the speaker, but only for a second. Then came the voice she expected to hear, in midsentence.

"...do you copy? Chief Sanders? Patrolman Martin? Respond, will you?"

Belle picked up the microphone. She would give herself away if she replied. But she needed to stall until she was over the hill. She pressed the mike switch several times, causing the speaker to crackle, hoping it would sound as if she were trying to answer.

"This is Deputy Tippet. I didn't quite copy that. Repeat please."

Belle pressed the switch several more times while saying in her best imitation of the young policeman at Bettenberg, "I didn't copy." She hoped the deputy would assume she was having radio problems and go back. But the cruiser kept coming.

A couple of tree-shrouded bends brought Belle to the crest. A mile or more ahead blazed the cherry-red lights of the ambulance. She wound down a curve and pulled off onto a gravel shoulder. Hopping out, she left the door open and ran several dozen yards up the slope to a spot where part of the bank at the side of the road had been washed away by erosion. Sliding down, she lay flat.

It wasn't long before the cruiser flew over the top and its headlights splashed over the police car. She heard the crunch of its tires, and cautiously raising her head, she saw the deputy pull in behind the Bettenberg vehicle. He got out and looked around in confusion.

"Chief Sanders? Martin? Where are you?"

Belle edged up the bank. The deputy had his back to her and was slowly advancing on the patrol car. He had placed a hand on the butt of his pistol.

"This is Deputy Tippet! Someone answer me!"

Reaching the top, Belle moved onto the asphalt where her short-heeled alligator skin shoes were whisper quiet. With a skill that came from being a tomboy when she was younger, she stalked her unsuspecting quarry.

Tippet reached the police car and poked his head inside. "What the hell?" Straightening, he stepped toward the front of the vehicle. "Someone answer me, damn it! Where are you?"

Belle placed each foot down with exquisite care. She came abreast of the deputy's cruiser and saw a shotgun inside. Unfortunately it was clamped to the dash. Bending low, she moved past the cruiser to the rear of the police car and ducked down.

Tippet was at the edge of the gravel, peering into the woods. "Martin, are you down there taking a whiz?" When he received no answer, he called out, "If this is another of your stupid jokes, I'm going to rip out your throat!"

Inching to the end of the fender, Belle peered over the trunk and saw the deputy come around the hood toward the open door. He leaned inside again and reached for the microphone.

In three bounds Belle reached him and jammed the muzzle of the Smith & Wesson against his ribs. "Leave it alone!" she ordered. "Back out slowly with your hands above your head."

Tippet stiffened and glanced over a shoulder. "What is this, lady? Who are you and what do you want?"

Belle thumbed back the hammer. "Ever seen the size of the hole a .44 Magnum round makes? I'd shut up, if I were you, and do exactly as I say."

His Adam's apple bobbing, Tippet complied.

The road was deserted in both directions. Belle grabbed him by the scruff of the neck and marched him over to the bank. His nerve broke when she pressed the revolver to the base of his skull.

"Wait, lady! Can't we talk this out! I've never done you any harm. And I have a wife at home."

"Do you think I care?" Belle said. She curled her finger around the trigger, then hesitated. Before her floated the image of the black-haired do-gooder who had saved her at the mansion, silent accusation in his ice-blue eyes. Snarling, she brought the revolver crashing down onto the back of deputy's head. He pitched down the incline, unconscious but alive, and slid to rest on his stomach.

Belle stared a moment, then whirled. "Damn you, Badass!" she fumed. "Damn you all to hell!"

13

LaPierre Street in Baton Rouge was a quaint tree-lined thoroughfare flanked by old brownstones. Nina's apartment was midway down the seven hundred block, on the third floor. Mack Bolan drove by without appearing to pay much notice to the building or the Buick parked across the street, but he didn't miss a thing. Two triggermen were in the front seat, another in the back. At the next corner he turned and went around the block.

At that hour the streets were largely deserted. Bolan parked the coupe but didn't get out right away. The last thing he needed was to have a police officer catch sight of him toting all his hardware. He stripped off his Kevlar vest and placed it on the back seat. His Desert Eagle and the grenades went under the front seat. He also shrugged out of his shoulder rig, tossed it in the back and wedged the Beretta under his belt.

Bending under the dash, the Executioner unwound the wires he had crossed to jump-start the car. He locked the other three doors and climbed out. Since it wouldn't do to leave the last door unlocked, even though he didn't have a key, he lowered the window just far enough to be able to slip his arm inside, then locked it.

A plank fence hemmed the small backyard to Nina's building. The latch in the gate creaked but not loud enough to be heard out front. A concrete walkway brought Bolan to the back door. Nina had promised him it would be unlocked, and she was true to her word.

Bolan slowly entered. A single dull bulb lit a narrow hall filled with a musty smell. The stairs were on the right. The soldier took them two at a stride. The third floor was as still as a tomb, but he didn't show himself until he had checked it from end to end.

Nina's apartment was 309. Bolan knocked on it but there was no response. He tapped again, a bit louder, with the same result. Not wanting to wake any of her neighbors by knocking, he pressed his mouth to the jamb and whispered her name.

"Is someone there?" Nina asked loud enough to be heard on the ground floor. "Who is it? What do you want?"

The woman had the discretion of a tabloid reporter. "It's me, Mike," Bolan whispered. "Let me in."

A bolt rasped, the door opened, and Nina flew into his arms and hugged him. "You're here! You're really here!" she squealed.

Clamping a hand over her mouth, Bolan whisked her inside, shut the door and threw the dead bolt. "Yell it from the rooftop, why don't you? The men in the car probably didn't hear."

"Oh." Nina grinned self-consciously and reluctantly

lowered her arms. "I was so glad to see you, I wasn't think-ing." Clasping his hand, she guided him into a musty liv-ing room overrun with knickknacks. "I can't tell you how worried I've been you wouldn't make it."

"Grab your suitcase. I'm getting you out."

"Out? I thought you would, like, kill them or something. I wasn't planning on leaving again. My suitcase is empty."

"You unpacked?" Bolan had to remind himself she had never been in a situation like this. He couldn't hold her lapses in judgment against her.

Nina gave him her little-girl grin. "I was bored sitting around here waiting. And I didn't have anything better to do."

"Then get your toothbrush and a change of clothes and we'll—" Bolan stopped and tilted his head. He thought he had heard a sound out in the hallway.

"What's wrong?" Nina asked.

The soldier placed a finger to his lips and glided toward the door. He had five or six feet to go when a floorboard creaked. Drawing the Beretta, he stopped.

Someone whispered, "Do it."

The door burst inward with a rending crash. Two of the gunners from the Buick had barreled into it shoulders-first. Their momentum pitched them onto the floor. The third killer sprang into the doorway. In his hands was an Ingram SMG fitted with a snub-nosed sound suppressor, and the instant he saw Bolan, he cut loose.

Bolan hurled himself backward half a step ahead of holes that sprouted along the wall. He fired as he moved, but his slug bit into the doorjamb. Reaching the living room, he spun and leaped—straight into Nina, who was rushing out to see what was happening. He couldn't keep his foot-ing and they both went down, Nina screaming in his ear.

Shoes pounded in the hall. The Executioner pushed her

off and rolled up onto a knee just as one of the gunners filled the living-room doorway. The man had a Ruger P-85 in each hand, and he blasted away with ambidextrous enthusiasm. His aim, though, wasn't the equal of his eagerness.

A flick of Bolan's finger switched the Beretta's selector switch to burst made, and he fired into the shooter's face. Heaving erect, he grabbed Nina by the arm and threw her toward the sofa. She squawked again as she slammed into it and toppled over.

The man with the Ingram stood in the doorway. His SMG swept from left to right, spewing lead like there was no tomorrow.

Bolan dived for the floor, his shoulder bearing the brunt. He got off another burst as he hit, but the wily gunner had dodged from sight. Scrambling behind a rocking chair, Bolan crouched and flipped down the grip in front of the Beretta's trigger guard. Adopting a two-handed grip, he extended the barrel between two of the chair's slats.

"Now!" someone bawled, and the remaining two triggermen charged into the living room shoulder to shoulder. The third man was armed with a SIG MP-310, firing a 9 mm Parabellum hailstorm. A .45 ACP deluge spouted from the other gunner's Ingram. Combined, their firepower was enough to reduce almost all the furniture to kindling in a span of seconds.

Bolan involuntarily recoiled as the top of the rocking chair shattered and half the slats dissolved into splinters. He unleashed two swift bursts but only one scored, clipping the Cajun with the SIG. The man buckled, and immediately his companion clamped onto him and they retreated around the corner.

The Executioner needed to change position. Flattening, he snaked to the opposite side of the room, to an easy chair that lay partly in pieces. On the wall nearby a painting hung in tatters. Thankfully Nina had the good sense to stay down and not utter a peep.

A cocking handle ratcheted, and the shooters rushed into the living room. They opened up as they crossed the threshold, their weapons chugging in unison. They sprayed the rocking chair, splintering it into fragments, then pivoted and began spraying everything from the floor to the ceiling and down again.

They hadn't spotted Bolan yet. They thought he was still near the rocking chair. The guy with the SIG was closer so Bolan drilled him first, two 3-round bursts that lifted the man off his feet and knocked him back against the wall where he oozed to the floor leaving a wide scarlet smear.

The last triggerman skipped backward, lead raining in sheets from the Ingram, and made it around the corner.

Bolan pressed the magazine release at the heel of the Beretta's grips, ejected the partially spent magazine and slapped in a fresh magazine, all in one smooth motion. Then he sprinted to the right, changing position yet again.

Out past the doorway there was the thud of the Ingram's magazine hitting the floor and the slap of a new one being shoved home.

It smelled like a shooting range in the living room. Mixed with the acrid scent was the pungent odor of freshly spilled blood. Bolan took one more step and crouched, the Beretta extended in front of him. It was do or die. He waited for the last gunner to make a move. He didn't wait long.

Into the living room flew the guy with the Ingram. His initial rounds were directed at the easy chair, where Bolan had last been. Realizing he had been outwitted, he swiveled, the Ingram belching nonstop.

Bolan fired, and with each burst the hardcase was jolted

backward. Howling in rage, the man crumpled, the Ingram chewing the floor with a few last rounds. In the sudden silence that ensued Bolan heard a woman on a lower floor screaming.

The police would soon be on their way.

"Nina, we have to get out of here!" Bolan urged, and when she didn't respond, he turned toward the sofa. Only then did he see the dozens of holes that had churned the upholstery to bits. With a cold sensation clawing at his insides he crossed the intervening space, leaned on the armrest and looked behind it.

"Hell." Bolan's shoulders slumped and he bowed his head. For long seconds he was motionless, until the distant wail of a siren roused him into reaching down and gently closing her eyes. "I'm sorry," he said softly.

IT WAS KNOWN AS the Crescent City, one of the great ports of the world. Billions of dollars' worth of exports and imports flowed through New Orleans every year. Vessels from around the globe docked at her wharves, bringing sugar, coffee, bananas and more. With its access to the Gulf of Mexico, and to points inland via the mighty Mississippi River, the city was ideally located for commerce.

It was also a smuggler's paradise. Thousands of cargo ships and lesser boats came into New Orleans yearly, and with them came untold millions in drugs and guns and every other illegal article under the sun. The Coast Guard and the port authorities couldn't possibly stem the tide, though they valiantly tried.

Which was all the better for the smuggler who ruled the roost. New Orleans was Carbou's home turf. He had been born and raised there. He knew the city inside and out. It was claimed he handled two-thirds of all the hard stuff that came through the bustling city.

All the more reason for the Executioner to want to put him out of business.

Bolan had been to New Orleans before and knew it fairly well. He took a room at a motel within sight of the Superdome, placed a call to Brognola to let the big Fed know where he was staying and turned in. He had been on the go for more than twenty-four hours, and he was worn out. Not bothering to turn the bedspread back, he plopped on the bed and lay on his stomach with his arm outflung.

Sleep wouldn't come right away. Bolan kept thinking about Nina. She had strayed off the straight and narrow, but basically she had been a decent person. Given the chance, she could have turned her life around and made something of herself. She would have made a great nurse.

Her mistake had been in taking the easy way out. When life offered her a choice between hard work and easy money, she chose the money. And she wasn't alone. Untold millions did the same every year. They knew what they were doing was wrong, but so long as they weren't hurting anyone except themselves, they figured it was all right.

Someone was knocking on the door.

With a start, Bolan sat up. According to the clock on the night stand, he had been asleep for eight hours. It was almost five o'clock. Holding the Beretta close to his leg, he crossed the room. Through the peephole he saw a young man in an off-the-rack suit. The guy had Fed written all over him. "What do you want?"

"Mr. Blanski, sir? Mr. Brognola asked me to deliver a bag of goodies, with his compliments, and your new wheels."

Bolan opened the door, careful not to show himself

fully. The man seemed legit, but it didn't pay to get sloppy. "Goodies?"

"I'm Agent Richards, sir. I was instructed to deliver this to you in person." Richards nodded at a bulging duffel bag behind him. It was secured with a lock. "I have no idea what's in it." He held out a key. "I was also ordered to give you this."

Good old Hal, Bolan thought. Palming the key, he gripped the duffel's carrying strap and hauled it inside. The thing had to weight upward of one hundred pounds. "Thank Brognola for me."

Richards was plainly burning with curiosity, but he had enough sense not to pry. "Will do, sir," he said and started to walk off. "Oh. I almost forgot. He said to tell you to be sure to look at the bottom."

Bolan closed the door. He swung the heavy bag onto the bed, unfastened the lock and began pulling out the contents. There was spare ammo for the Beretta and the Desert Eagle. There was a new M-16, stripped down into the upper and lower receiver groups. There was another 40 mm M-203 grenade launcher. There was C-4, det cord and timers. Several knives and a dagger, field rations, an assortment of grenades, a crisp, clean blacksuit and a folded trench coat.

The item that interested Bolan the most, though, was one he hadn't expected. Brognola had thrown in a surprise, a USM-40 A-1 sniper rifle in a compact case. Essentially a military version of the Remington Model 700 sporting rifle, this model was chambered for the 7.62 mm NATO cartridge. It was a favorite of the Marines. Attached to it was a conventional top-quality scope.

Toward the bottom of the duffel was a backpack, a first-aid kit, a packet of combat cosmetics, a coil of rope, a grappling hook, binoculars and a packet of maps. The top map was of New Orleans. Unfolding it, Bolan saw where Brognola had marked three spots with bright red Xs.

As if on cue, the phone rang. Bolan snagged it and quipped, "Christmas came early this year."

"I was going to include a fruitcake, but it wouldn't fit," the big Fed responded. "You've seen the map?"

"Looking at it as we speak." Bolan noted the locations of the Xs. "My guess is the waterfront address is where the drugs come in. The Canal Street office is a front for contacting his suppliers." He tapped the last red X. "Five will get you ten the third address is a ritzy house he owns under an alias." Smugglers weren't any different from drug lords and other criminals rolling in money. They liked to flash their wealth around and savor the fruits of their ill-gotten gains.

"Maybe you should consider starting your own psychic network," Brognola said. "Every guess was right on the money." He paused. "The thing is, Carbou probably has more haunts we don't know about. It could take a month to track him down."

"Or I could get lucky first time up to the plate." Bolan placed the map on the dresser and sat on the bed. "Either way, I'm not leaving until I nail him."

"I'm sorry about the woman," Brognola mentioned. "I had my people contact her sister and her aunt, but they want nothing to do with her. They want her buried in a pauper's grave, I'm afraid."

"No, she won't. I want a decent headstone. At my expense."

"You can't blame yourself."

"Tell that to my conscience." Bolan hung up and strode into the bathroom. He never should have let Nina go into the bar with him. He had used her as cover, and it ultimately led to her murder.

Turning on the shower, Bolan stripped and stepped into the stall. The cold water brought goose bumps to his skin. He faced into the spray and stood still for the longest while, composing himself. When he emerged, his rock-hard muscles glistening, the self-reproach in his eyes was gone. He had come to terms with his guilt. There was a war to fight. It took precedence over all else, including his personal feelings.

Bolan dried himself and donned the blacksuit. His shoulder rig went under his right arm. He strapped the holstered Desert Eagle to his waist and a knife in a Velcro sheath to his right ankle. Odds and ends completed his collection. Finally he shrugged into the black trench coat.

The soldier replaced every item except the map of New Orleans and the sniper rifle in the duffel bag. He attached the lock, hefted the bag over his shoulder, slipped the map into a pocket, and, with the rifle under his left arm, went out into the humid New Orleans night.

The coupe was gone. Parked in the exact same parking space was a new Chevy Blazer. The keys were where Brognola usually had his people leave them, in a small metal container affixed to the front fender well on the driver's side.

Bolan tossed the bag into the rear compartment, laid the rifle case on the back seat and went to work.

CANAL STREET WAS the hub of New Orleans's business district. Bolan drove north, noting the building numbers. Off to the right was the French Quarter. He passed department stores and smaller shops, and throngs of pedestrians jamming the sidewalks.

The address turned out to be six-story modern complex devoted entirely to commercial enterprises. On the fourth floor was Metarie Imports. A spacious reception area was presided over by a pert young secretary who smiled warmly as Bolan entered. She greeted him with a cheery, "Good evening, sir. How may I help you?" Then she quickly added, as if afraid his visit would entail overtime on her part, "It's almost six, and we're about to close up for the day."

"Is Mr. Carbou in?" Bolan asked.

"Who? I'm afraid that name doesn't ring a bell."

Bolan believed her. Carbou wouldn't be stupid enough to use his real name. "Who is in charge here?"

"You mean the president of the company? That would be Mr. Metarie, naturally. He's in, but he doesn't see anyone without an appointment." The secretary plucked a pen from a holder and poised it over a notepad. "If I can have your name and number, he'll get back to you as soon as he can."

"That won't be necessary," Bolan said and drew the Beretta. "Do me a favor and show me into his office. But be quiet. I want it to be a surprise."

The secretary tried to say something, but her vocal cords wouldn't work. Nodding vigorously, she stiffly rose and backed toward a mahogany door. She groped for the handle without looking, twisted and continued backing into the room.

"Ms. Lahane? What's the meaning of this?"

Bolan angled to the left and trained the Beretta on a portly man behind an ornate desk. "I didn't want her phoning the police while my back was turned."

Metarie, if that was his real name, had the appearance of a typical businessman, but he didn't react with surprise or outrage as genuine a businessman would.

"I want you to give Lafe Carbou a message for me," Bolan directed.

"I don't believe I know the gentleman."

"Maybe this will refresh your memory." Bolan sent a slug into a computer monitor the man had been studying. The screen shattered and sparks flew as thick as fireflies.

Metarie recoiled, a hand to his face.

"Did it help?" Bolan asked.

The president of Carbou's front company glowered, his pudgy fingers clawed. "I still don't know who you are referring to," he said defiantly.

Bolan fired into the computer itself, two swift shots that sent metal and plastic slivers flying and caused the unit to crackle and sputter. Tiny wisps of smoke arose. "I hope Carbou appreciates how loyal you are."

Metarie's thick lips worked, but no sounds came out.

"Tell your boss I'll be back," Bolan said. "Tell him killing Rabican didn't solve his problems. It compounded them." He sidestepped to the door and winked at the horrified secretary. "You might want to look for a new job. This company won't be in business much longer."

PONCHATOULA SHIPPING, Incorporated listed offices in Brisbane, Istanbul and Bogotá on the sign out front. Longshoremen were unloading a freighter at berth at a dock adjoining the huge warehouse. A tiny bell tinkled as Bolan opened the door to the main office. Instead of a pretty secretary, a large man in longshoreman's garb looked up from a girlie magazine he was reading and demanded, "What do you want?"

"I was hoping to see Mr. Hyde," Bolan said amiably. That was the name listed as company president.

"He's not in," the man said, returning to the magazine. "We're closed, anyway. Come back tomorrow morning at eight."

"You wouldn't be lying to me, would you, King Kong?"

"What did you just call me?" Three hundred pounds of raw muscle heaved up out of the chair and the magazine fluttered to the floor. "Are you some kind of smart guy? Get out before I break you over my knee."

"I insist on seeing Hyde," Bolan said, producing the Beretta.

The hardman blinked and partially deflated. "You must be crazy. Do you have any idea who runs this outfit?"

"Why do you think I'm here?" Bolan wagged the machine pistol at a door beyond the chair. Emblazoned on the glass in bright told letters was Charles Hyde, CEO. "After you. Nice and slow, if you don't mind."

"You're dead meat, mister," the man declared, but he did as he had been told and dutifully went on in.

Bolan was on a roll. The man who called himself Charles Hyde was in. A bean-pole with a pencil-thin mustache, an expensive suit and the haughty air of a street thug, Hyde had his feet propped on his desk and was staring out over the harbor. Glancing around, he leaped up and demanded, "What the hell is going on here?"

"I have a message for your employer," the soldier said and fired at an overhead fluorescent light. It burst with a loud pop. Bits of glass showered onto the wine-red carpet, and onto Hyde. "Tell him I'm after him. Tell him I'll be back."

Hyde gestured at the large man. "Is this what you're paid to do, Folson? Stand there like a bump on a log while some bozo threatens me?"

Just like that, Folson spun, his hand dipping under his jacket and reappearing with a bowie knife. He was fast for someone his size but not fast enough to dodge the slug that cored his thigh and buckled him onto his knees.

"Lose it," Bolan directed, and when Folson tossed the knife into a far corner, he circled over to the desk.

Hyde was nervous but striving not to show it. "What are you up to?"

"Amending my message," Bolan said and slugged him across the temple with the Beretta.

Hyde stumbled against his chair, tripped and keeled to the floor. He tried to rise, groaned once, then passed out.

Folson shook his head as the Executioner made for the doorway. "Do you have any idea what you've just done?"

Bolan nodded and backed out. He knew exactly what he was up to. Sometimes the best way to intimidate an enemy into making a tactical blunder was to forewarn them. He wanted Lafe Carbou to sweat. He wanted Carbou's whole organization in turmoil. Most of all, he wanted Carbou to divert men to Metarie Imports and Ponchatoula Shipping, leaving fewer gunners where Carbou would need them most.

Next stop: Carbou's house.

14

Located in an affluent neighborhood where swimming pools graced every yard and three-car garages were the norm, Carbou's house radiated luxury. A newer addition, it also boasted a flower-bedecked gazebo in the backyard, a small guest house at the rear and a high wall covered with ivy.

Several hundred yards to the south, braked at a stop sign, the Executioner swept his binoculars from east to west and back again. Finding a vantage point to snipe from was a challenge. The adjacent properties were flat and open with little in the way of vegetation. Carbou's property was only two and a half acres, and there wasn't a tree anywhere.

Bolan centered the binoculars on the guest house and adjusted the focus. It sat at right angles to the main house, was only a single story and had a V-shaped roof. Someone lying on the far side wouldn't be visible to those in the main house but would have an unobstructed view of its rear windows and most of those on the south side. He'd found his vantage point.

The horizon had devoured the sun, but night had yet to descend. Bolan dropped the binoculars onto the seat and drove on. He rode by the front gate, noting the exodus taking place. A black limo was being backed out of the third garage port, and six hardmen were waiting to pile in. Three more hired guns were over by the front door. But Carbou hadn't posted guards at the gate itself. Too obvious, Bolan guessed, for someone trying to keep a low profile.

The soldier drove a quarter of a mile and took a right. He had time to kill. Driving through the neighborhood again might attract unwanted attention, so he took scenic Lakeshore Drive and followed it along the shore of Lake Pontchartrain. At the east end was an amusement park. Wheeling into the parking lot, he parked facing the lake so if he was being tailed he would know it.

Five minutes later Bolan turned to the back seat and grabbed the sniper rifle. The windows were tinted, so he wasn't worried about passersby seeing in. The M-40 A-1 had been broken down to fit into the compact hardwood case. He had to replace the bolt assembly and attach the scope. Three magazines were included. Bolan fed five cartridges into each, slapped one into the rifle and pocketed the spares.

Bolan glanced at the duffel bag. He had enough C-4 in there to bring the house crashing down around Carbou's ears, but he didn't dare risk using high explosives in a residential area. The same went for the hand grenades. This was a sniping op only.

Stars were twinkling when Bolan started the Blazer and returned to Casa Estates. He parked a good five hundred yards from Carbou's. Sliding the rifle under his trench coat, he came up on the rear of the property by a round-about route. The wall was eight feet high, but the ivy made scaling it a breeze. Lying on his belly on top, he sought signs of Carbou's triggermen.

The backyard was splashed by rectangles of light from the windows in the main house, so he could tell the gazebo was empty. A spotlight revealed the heart-shaped pool was deserted. And the guest house was pitch-black inside.

Bolan couldn't ask for a sweeter setup. Grasping the rifle in his left hand, he crawled to the corner, then along the south wall until he was only six feet from the guest-house roof. Rising onto a knee, he slung the sniper rifle.

Six feet wasn't much of a jump unless it had to be done without a running start. Bolan slowly rose, keeping his knees tucked, and inched to the brink. He checked the main house once more, insuring no one was at the windows. Then, girding himself, he leaped.

For a millisecond the soldier hung in space. His shoes came down hard on the shingles, and he threw himself flat to keep from sliding. Gravity wouldn't be denied, and he slid toward the bottom edge. He had to claw at the shingles and dig his shoes in hard to stop himself from falling off.

Quickly sitting up, Bolan unslung the sniper rifle and listened. No outcries had been raised. No shots rang out. Snaking to the top, he peered over. He could see people moving in some of the rooms. Sculpting the scope to his right eye, he tweaked it for the proper magnification and began ranging it over the windows.

That was when the ivy rustled.

Bolan glanced over a shoulder. The rustling was re-peated, and a moment later a gloved hand appeared, clutching the top of the rear wall. With nowhere else to go, he rolled up and over the roof's crest and swiveled onto his stomach. It exposed him to view from the main house, but it couldn't be helped. Cautiously he raised an eye to the crest.

Another hand now gripped the wall. A head poked above the rim, smeared with camouflage cosmetics, and a lanky man swung up and lay in almost the exact spot Bolan had occupied a minute ago. An M-16 was slung across his right shoulder. He surveyed the backyard, then bent toward the street and extended his left arm. Seconds later a broad-shouldered man was on top of the wall with him. Both wore fatigues and were armed to the gills.

Who in the world? Bolan wondered. And it hit him. They fit Brognola's description of the Scorpion Killers. It was Ryker and Winslow, the pair selected by Considine to eliminate the Scorpions. They wouldn't be there unless they were expecting the Scorpions to show up. And like him, the pair was going for the only decent sniping spot within six blocks, the roof of the guest house.

Bolan had just put two and two together before all hell broke loose.

Somewhere in the main house a woman screamed. A gun thundered and was answered by the rattle of an SMG. More guns boomed, accompanied by a riot of yells and oaths. A window blew out with a loud crash.

But Bolan couldn't look to see what was going on. First he had the Scorpion Killers to deal with. Winslow had risen and helped Ryker to stand, and they were hurrying around the wall toward the point where he had leaped to the roof. They were in a rush to get into position, and in their haste didn't spot him.

Bolan could easily pick them off, but he remembered

what Brognola had said. Ryker and Winslow weren't assassins. They weren't part of the death squad. They were unwitting dupes in a scheme concocted by Considine to cover his butt if things went wrong. To Brognola's knowledge they sincerely thought they were working for the U.S. government. He couldn't simply shoot them.

Winslow reached the spot where they had to jump. Ryker, hobbled by his bad knee, was just rounding the corner. The former SEAL's left leg couldn't bend thanks to a pair of metal rods where his kneecap had been. Winslow beckoned, and Ryker motioned for him to make the jump first.

The battle in the main house was spreading. Bolan tore his gaze from the Scorpion Killers long enough to witness women and children fleeing down a hall and six or seven of Carbou's shooters engaged in a running firefight with three figures in combat gear. Apparently the Scorpions were out for Carbou's blood. It made no sense, especially since it was Carbou who hired them to kill Rabican. There had been a falling out of some kind.

A thump on the other side of the guest-house roof reminded Bolan he had a problem of his own. If Ryker and Winslow caught sight of him, they'd mistake him for one of Carbou's boys and open fire without giving him a chance to explain. Unless he took them out without doing them serious harm.

Winslow made the leap and turned to the wall. "I'll grab you," he whispered, holding out his right hand.

Flexing his good leg, Ryker gauged the distance. "Don't miss," he said. Holding both arms well out in front of him, he pushed off with his good leg.

Lunging, Winslow succeeded in wrapping a hand around his partner's wrist, but he couldn't manage the leverage needed to swing him onto the roof. Ryker dangled over the side, kicking at the wall with his left leg in an attempt to gain purchase. Winslow, grunting, strained to hold on.

Bolan was over the crest and halfway down the roof before either realized he was there. Winslow heard him and clawed for a pistol with his other hand. Ryker tried to bring his M-16 to bear. Both were a shade too slow. Bolan slammed the butt of his rifle into Winslow's temple and the African-American was pitched over the edge, taking Ryker with him.

Bolan glanced down. Winslow was out cold on top of Ryker, who was dazedly struggling to free himself. "Get out of here!" Bolan called down. "The man who hired you wasn't what he seemed to be."

That was all Bolan had time to say. Shifting toward the main house, he raised the sniper rifle. Bodies lay all over the place, in hallways, in various rooms, on a stairway. Gunners who had been riddled with bullets, women lying in crimson pools, even a child sprawled over a couch.

It was a slaughter. The Scorpions were killing everyone, just like at Rabican's. They had to be stopped.

Bolan swept the scope from window to window. He saw a gunner stagger along a corridor, hands pressed to a bloody chest. A woman and several children were huddled behind a dresser in an upstairs bedroom. But of the Scorpions, and Carbou, there was no sign.

Suddenly the patio door on the north side crashed open and out backed a dozen hardmen, frantically firing into the house. They had formed a protective ring around their employer and were trying to usher him to safety. Their goal was a small gate in the fence on the north side of the pool. But to reach it they had to cross a lot of open ground.

A gunner near the house grabbed at his chest and fell. Another screamed as holes pockmarked his face.

Carbou was screaming, "Get them! Get them!" in rising desperation.

Bolan focused on the window to the room flanking the patio. The furniture was being blown to pieces, and a mirror showered down in slivers. He couldn't see the Scorpions. They had to be low to the floor.

Shifting, Bolan trained his scope on Lafe Carbou, and the smuggler's beefy, florid features filled the crosshairs. He couldn't permit the smuggler to get away. Every pimple, every bead of sweat, stood out in stark relief. Bolan sucked in a hasty breath to steady his body, and his aim.

Carbou turned toward the far fence. His face registered shock, and his mouth grew slack. Pointing, he yelled something to his men.

Bolan raised his head a hair. A new element had intruded itself. More hardboiled shooters were streaming through the small gate, but they weren't Carbou's men. They were led by a blond Valkyrie dressed in black and wielding a pistol-grip shotgun with deadly efficiency. It was Belle, out to avenge her husband.

The Executioner molded his right eye to the scope again, but Carbou's image no longer filled it.

The smuggler and his surviving bodyguards had changed direction and were barreling across the backyard toward the gazebo. Under fire from the house and from Belle and her men, they were being cut to ribbons. Only seven were left.

An SMG opened up from the window by the patio. Bolan fixed his rifle on a dark-haired thatch of hair and recognized Rico Fuentes. The Scorpion was grinning in feral delight. He was concealed from Carbou's men but not from the roost atop the guest house. Bolan aimed at a spot half an inch above Fuentes's right eye. Again he held his breath, again he lightly touched his finger to the trigger. And smoothly squeezed.

The shot was dead on. Fuentes was propelled backward onto the floor, the rear of his cranium smearing the tile. His thin lips drawn back, he broke into convulsions. They didn't last long. His right hand started to rise but went limp. His whole body deflated, and he was still.

Bolan turned his attention back to Carbou. The smuggler and his remaining men had reached the gazebo and were crouched behind it, returning fire. Bolan tried to fix the scope on the back of Carbou's head, but an ornate bench was in the way. He couldn't get a clear shot.

Belle and her shooters had spread out and sought cover behind lawn chairs, trash cans and whatever else was handy. She had lost several men in the charge on the pool, and now another tumbled to the ground.

The firing from the main house had ceased. Bolan looked for Culver and Carson, but the Scorpions weren't anywhere to be seen. They were either moving to new positions, or they were vacating the premises. He considered jumping down and going after them. Two factors dissuaded him. He couldn't cross the backyard without drawing a withering cross fire from the gazebo and Bell's bunch. And if the Scorpions were leaving, they would be long gone before he reached the front of the house.

A second later a third factor reared its unforeseen head.

Someone began firing at the gazebo from the front corner of the guest house. Quickly Bolan crawled to the south edge.

Winslow was still unconscious, but Ryker had pushed out from under him and inexplicably added his M-16 to the din. Maybe he was worried Carbou's bunch would retreat to the guest house next. He had dropped a goon, but others were keeping him pinned down with a steady peppering of autofire.

Bolan wished Ryker had taken his advice. The Scorpion Killers had no business getting involved. Suddenly Winslow groaned and stirred and lurched erect. Cupping a hand to his mouth, Bolan was about to shout for them to get out of there when rounds thudded into the roof inches above his head. He flattened, thinking perhaps he had been spotted by one of Carbou's gunners in the back yard.

The Executioner carefully rose onto his elbows. The gunners at the gazebo were either engaged with Belle's strike force or were exchanging shots with Ryker and Winslow. He looked for Carbou but couldn't spot him.

Suddenly the back door to the main house flew open. Out hurtled Culver and Carson, doubled over and firing on the fly. They made for a shed near the south fence. Carson raked Belle's men while Culver concentrated on the gazebo, forcing both groups to hug dirt. They reached the shed intact and darted behind it.

Chaos ensued. The Scorpions, the Scorpion Killers, Belle's men and Carbou's gunners all fired at one another in a wild leaden melee. As if that weren't enough, someone on the second floor of the house joined the madness, cutting loose with an Uzi. Given the number of wild shots being thrown, it was only a matter of time before people in adjoining homes were clipped by stray rounds.

Time to end it. Bolan rested the sniper rifle on the crest and aimed at one of the four shooters still crouched behind the gazebo. He stroked the trigger, smoothly worked the bolt and stroked the trigger again. He kept firing until the magazine was empty, and when he was done, the four flunkies lay in spreading pools of their own blood.

Bolan ejected the spent magazine and inserted his first spare. The Scorpions were too well hidden behind the shed, so he swiveled toward the pool area. He had lost sight of Belle, but six of her Cajun killers were still ranged across the lawn. Aiming at the man on the left, Bolan fired, worked the bolt, fired at the next of her hardmen, worked the bolt and fired at a third prone shooter. With each blast a man cried out or went limp or flopped about like a fish out of water. Five shots, in all. Five killers dead.

The last of Belle's boys shoved upright and bolted for the small gate, but a short burst from the shed sent him cartwheeling into the pool.

Ejecting the second magazine, Bolan smacked home the third and swung toward the shed, hoping for a clear shot. The Scorpion responsible had ducked back down. He started to search for Carbou and Belle when a scrabbling noise from a few yards to his left alerted him to movement on the south wall.

Winslow had jumped up and caught hold of the top of the wall with one arm. Now he was leveling his M-16 at the shed with the other. He probably thought Culver and Carson wouldn't spot him there deep in the shadows, but he was wrong.

Culver popped up and fired on full-auto. Miniature dust devils spurted as heavy slugs chewed a path toward the former SWAT sniper. Winslow let go of the wall and attempted to drop back down, but the slugs caught him in midair, coring him from his chest to his crotch. He was flipped to earth in a heap.

"No!" The cry came from Ryker.

Bolan trained his rifle on Culver, but she ducked before

he could nail her. The guy with the Uzi at the second-floor window had seen her, too, and opened fire again. The Executioner had a clear shot, but he didn't take the guy down. Not when the Uzi-wielder might bag Culver and Carson. Putting an end to the Scorpions took precedence over all else.

Someone else thought so, too. Ryker poured in lead from the corner of the guest house. Between them, he and the guy with the Uzi were turning the shed into a sieve. Then both weapons went empty, and in the seconds it took them to feed in new magazines, the Scorpions burst from cover.

Culver hurled a metallic object at the main house. Carson threw a similar object at the guest house.

It didn't take a genius to figure out what. Bolan had started to fix his scope on Culver but instead he spun, raced to the opposite end of the roof and leaped without looking. The ground was still several feet below him when the night resounded with twin explosions. A sledgehammer wall of air and a deluge of slivers buffeted Bolan's back, and he was tossed like a rag doll.

With an agile flip, the soldier rolled up into a crouch, the sniper rifle jammed to his shoulder. A jagged cavity existed where the second-floor window had been. Culver and Carson were rounding the heart-shaped pool, heading for the north fence.

Bolan sprinted across the yard in pursuit. He glanced back to check on Ryker and saw the Scorpion Killer's head and shoulders lying amid a pile of debris. *Just* the head and shoulders. The rest of him had been obliterated by Carson's grenade.

Bolan yearned to snap off a shot but couldn't. The Scorpions made it through the gate. He assumed they were racing for their vehicle so they could get out of there before the police arrive. But then he heard a pistol crack to the northeast, punctuated by the blast of a shotgun.

Only one person that Bolan knew of had been armed with a hand howitzer—Belle Rabican. And he could think of only one person she might be after—Lafe Carbou. Somehow the smuggler had gotten over the wall, and Belle had gone after him. Now the two Scorpions were after them.

Bolan ran faster. He kept one eye on the main house and another on the widely scattered bodies. Any one of the gunners might still be alive and tempted to stop him. He saw one of Belle's Cajuns move, but the man rose only a couple of inches, then collapsed.

Once through the gate Bolan devoted himself to overtaking the Scorpions. It opened into another yard. A husband, wife and two children had their pale faces pressed to a bay window. The small boy jabbed a finger at Bolan. The father shouted that the police were on their way.

A second shotgun blast gave the Executioner a direction to travel. He crossed the yard catty-corner, climbed over the fence and sprinted along a darkened side street. Up ahead were two dim forms. He paced himself, and five blocks later saw the Scorpions veer toward a cluster of bushes hemming a streetlight. When he got there, he discovered the bushes actually fringed a city park.

Sirens screamed to the south and the west. It would take the police minutes yet to reach Carbou's house, and by the time they sorted everything out and patrol cars were dispatched to scour the neighborhood, Bolan expected to be long gone. He plunged into the park and was swallowed by welcome darkness. To the northwest a pistol cracked. Again a shotgun answered, and a shriek wafted on the wind. Belle had shot Carbou.

An abrupt thought spurred Bolan into running flat-out. Belle didn't know the Scorpions were after Carbou and her. She would think it was finished and lower her guard. Bolan believed the shots came from about two hundred yards away, and he had covered half of them when self-preservation slowed him to a jog.

Fifty yards away was another streetlight. A figure appeared, strolling cheerfully along. It was Belle, grinning broadly, the pistol-grip shotgun resting casually across her left shoulder.

The very instant Bolan spied her, an SMG barked. He saw her jarred backward, saw the shotgun fall. As she staggered from the circle of light, two camouflage-clad shapes ran toward her.

Bolan flew toward the spot where they disappeared and heard the sounds of a scuffle. He came up behind them unnoticed. Carson was in back of Belle, holding her arms. Culver was in front of her, wagging a doubled-edged knife.

Bolan dropped the sniper rifle. A snap shot might go completely through Culver into Belle. Drawing the Beretta, he slowed even more to take better aim.

Even as he did, Culver declared, "This is for what your friend did to Placer," and thrust the blade into Belle's abdomen.

By then Bolan was on top of them. Culver whirled, cocking the bloody knife. He shot her from point-blank range, a 3-round burst that slammed her off her feet. But he couldn't fire at Carson with Belle held between them. He sidestepped for a clear shot, and the big soldier shoved her against him. Bolan caught her with his left arm, but he wasn't fully braced and it knocked him off his feet.

Carson took a step toward Culver, roaring, "Nooo!" Pivoting, he began to unsling his M-249.

Flat on his back with Belle lying across his legs, Bolan fired twice into the towering figure. Carson tottered and the M-249 dropped, but he stayed erect. Bolan fired again. This time the former soldier's knees gave way and he fell onto his side.

"Belle?" Bolan sat up and eased her off his legs. She was doubled over, her teeth clenched tight, her eyes shut. He rose onto a knee to examine her.

The thud of combat boots warned Bolan he had been premature. He whirled, but Carson was on him before he could snap off a shot. It was like being rammed into by a bulldozer. He wound up on his back again with Carson on top. The Beretta was wrenched from his grasp and fingers as thick as railroad spikes clamped onto his throat.

"You killed her!" the ex-Ranger railed.

Bolan groped for the Desert Eagle, but Carson's knee had it pinned to his side. He levered upward, seeking to throw Carson off, but the soldier wasn't to be denied. The fingers around his neck constricted, choking off his breath.

"You killed the woman I love!"

The Executioner drove a straight-arm punch into Carson's jaw, a blow that would have rendered most men senseless. But all it did was fuel Carson's fury, and his steely fingers dug deeper. Bolan swung again, shattering Carson's nose. It had no effect whatsoever. The soldier was beside himself.

Bolan surged upward once more. Carson clung on, berserk madness lighting his eyes, a snarl issuing from his contorted lips. Suddenly Carson's forehead erupted in a spray of blood, bone and flesh. Bolan shoved the heavy body off, got his hands under him and rose.

Belle was lying beside Culver. She had Culver's pistol, and she was smiling. "I owed you one, Badass," she said softly. The pistol fell. She cried out, her hand reaching for him.

Bolan grabbed it and eased her head onto his lap. Her gaze met his, and her grip tightened.

"Another time, another place, eh? Life can be so unfair, no?" Belle raised a blood-caked finger to his cheek and died.

After a moment Bolan gently lowered her to the grass. He folded her arms across her chest and straightened her curled legs. Slowly he rose and collected his weapons. He lingered a moment more, long enough to say, "Yes, it can." Then, squaring his shoulders, he jogged off into the night.

James Axler
Outlanders

SEA OF PLAGUE

The loyalties that united the Cerberus warriors have become undone, as a bizarre messenger from the future provides a look into encroaching horror and death. Kane and his band have one option: fix two fatal fault lines in the time continuum—and rewrite history before it happens. But first they must restore power to the barons who dare to defy the greater evil: the mysterious new Imperator. Then they must wage war in the jungles of India, where the deadly, beautiful Scorpia Prime and her horrifying bio-weapon are about to drown the world in a sea of plague....

In the Outlands, the shocking truth is humanity's last hope.

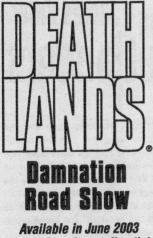

Take
2 explosive books
plus a
mystery bonus
FREE

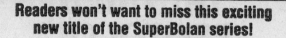

Readers won't want to miss this exciting new title of the SuperBolan series!

Don Pendleton's Mack Bolan

Line of Control

The powerful Kung Lok triad has set its sights on controlling the U.S. narcotics market. Backed by Hong Kong's underworld, they have the money, influence and bloodlust to get a foothold in the West by destroying the competition—a Mexican cartel equally determined to solidify its hold on the border pipeline. Mack Bolan's mission: keep the destruction to a minimum...and keep the bloodshed to the enemy.

Available in July 2003 at your favorite retail outlet.

Stony Man is deployed against an armed
invasion on American soil...

THE THIRD
PROTOCOL

As the violence in the Holy Land reaches critical mass,
the Arab world readies to involve itself militarily in the
conflict between Israel and the Palestinians. Only Stony Man
and the Oval Office understand the true horror behind the
bloodshed: a decades-old conspiracy and a plan involving
highly trained, well-equipped, well-funded moles, planted
in every Arab nation, now activated for the final act—
nuking the Middle East into oblivion.

STONY
MAN

*Available in
June 2003
at your favorite
retail outlet.*